CANVAS BLEEDING

Other Books by Michael Bracken

Fiction
All White Girls
Bad Girls
Deadly Campaign
Even Roses Bleed
In the Town of Dreams Unborn and Memories Dying
Just in Time for Love
Psi Cops
Tequila Sunrise
Fedora: Private Eyes and Tough Guys (editor)

CANVAS BLEEDING

Michael Bracken

WILDSIDE PRESS
Doylestown, Pennsylvania

Copyright © 2002 Michael Bracken.
All rights reserved.

"Legacy" first appeared in *Thin Ice* X, 1991. Copyright © 1991 by Michael Bracken.

"Of Memories Dying" first appeared in *Midnight*, edited by Charles L. Grant, Tor Books, 1985. Copyright © 1985 by Michael Bracken.

"The Seasons of Their Lives" first appeared in *Beyond the Rose* 6, 2001. Copyright © 2001 by Michael Bracken.

"Dead Air Days" first appeared in *New Texas 2001*, edited by Donna Walker-Nixon and James Ward Lee, University of Mary Hardin-Baylor, 2001. Copyright © 2001 by Michael Bracken.

"In the Death Ward" first appeared in *Thin Ice* XVII, 1995. Copyright © 1995 by Michael Bracken.

"Mermaid" is original to this volume. Copyright © 2002 by Michael Bracken.

"Karl and the Shadow Box" first appeared in *Weirdbook* 25, 1990. Copyright © 1990 by Michael Bracken.

"The Passenger" first appeared in *Fantasy Macabre* 8, 1986. Copyright © 1986 by Michael Bracken.

"Fine Print" first appeared in *Night Voyages* 10, 1984. Copyright © 1984 by Michael Bracken.

"Heirloom" first appeared in the Spring, 1982, issue of *Shadows Of*. Copyright © 1982 by Michael Bracken.

"The Man at the Window" first appeared in *Abrupt Darkness*, edited by Michael Thomas Dillon, Grafic Publishing, 1996. Copyright © 1996 by Michael Bracken.

"Father's Day" is original to this volume. Copyright © 2002 by Michael Bracken.

"All the World's a Rage" is original to this volume. Copyright © 2002 by Michael Bracken.

"Shadow of My Father" first appeared in *Northern Horror*, edited by Edo van Belkom, Quarry Press, 2000. Copyright © 2000 by Michael Bracken.

"A Thigh for a Thigh" first appeared in the November, 1987, issue of *Max* as "Time to Play, Time to Pay." Copyright © 1987 by Michael Bracken. It has been modified for inclusion in this volume.

"To Sleep, Perchance to Die" is original to this volume. Copyright © 2002 by Michael Bracken.

"Voices" is original to this volume. Copyright © 2002 by Michael Bracken.

"Soul Man" first appeared in the June 24, 2000, issue of *Dark Matter Chronicles*. Copyright © 2000 by Michael Bracken.

"What Little Girls Are Made Of" is original to this volume. Copyright © 2002 by Michael Bracken.

"Feeding Mary Ellen" is original to this volume. Copyright © 2002 by Michael Bracken.

"Something I Did with My Hands" is original to this volume. Copyright © 2002 by Michael Bracken.

"With Skin So Pale and Canvas Bleeding" is original to this volume. Copyright © 2002 by Michael Bracken.

"Fat Chicks Must Die" first appeared in *Delirium Magazine* 5, 2001. Copyright © 2001 by Michael Bracken.

"Violent Eyes" first appeared in *Aberrations* 31, 1995. Copyright © 1995 by Michael Bracken.

Canvas Bleeding
A publication of
Wildside Press
P.O. Box 301
Holicong, PA 18928-0301

www.wildsidepress.com

FIRST EDITION

Ryan, Ian, Courtney, *and* **Nigel:**
beware of things that go bump in the night

Table of Contents

Legacy	9
Of Memories Dying	11
The Seasons of Their Lives	19
Dead Air Days	25
In the Death Ward	31
Mermaid	35
Karl and the Shadow Box	37
The Passenger	49
Fine Print	59
Heirloom	67
The Man at the Window	77
Father's Day	83
All the World's a Rage	95
Shadow of My Father	107
A Thigh for a Thigh	111
To Sleep, Perchance to Die	123
Voices	129
Soul Man	137
What Little Girls Are Made Of	141
Feeding Mary Ellen	151
Something I Did with My Hands	157
With Skin So Pale and Canvas Bleeding	163
Fat Chicks Must Die	169
Violent Eyes	179

Legacy

Vampire parents
suck pain
like blood

using lamp cords
coat hangers
and fists

invited in
by children who've
no cross to bear

Of Memories Dying

*I*t was a small town on the northern California coast where the teenagers still cruised Main Street, stopping at both the stoplights on their trek from the A&W north to the bowling alley, then around and back again; a small town nestled against the ocean where the Coast Ranges prevented most radio and television signals from bringing in the latest fashions; a small town where progress rarely interfered and the A&W was still the only link to a world of fast food.

A full moon hung low in the evening sky, fragmented by naked power branches and power lines. I stood in the shadows before the high school, staring at the faded spot on the wall where the capital *B* had fallen off, leaving only *aker High School* still intact. The

Michael Bracken

school was much the same as it had been when I left, still a collection of single-story hallways intersecting to form inaccessible open courtyards.

I stood on a brown patch of grass, my knapsack at my feet. Faded green canvas, I'd bought it at an Army surplus store and carried it around the world with me, stuffing it with tiny objects I'd found in small villages and back-alley shops where tourists never went.

A breeze from the ocean blew up through town and sent a chill crawling through me. I pulled my jacket tighter around my gaunt frame, fumbling to tug the zipper upward with shaking fingers.

My clothes hung limply from my body, mismatched and out of style. The shirt, brown cotton gauze stained with sweat, I'd found in India. The jeans, now faded and frayed at the cuffs of the bell bottoms, were a pair of counterfeit Levi's I'd found in Hong Kong. The green jacket I'd received from an Army deserter in Cambodia after spending a five-day drunk with him, helping him through a bad case of the DT's and a good case of scotch. My shoes — a pair of low-top black tennis shoes — were new. I deserved that; I'd walked through the soles of so many others.

"Hey there!"

I was suddenly pinned against the school wall by a spotlight, silhouetted like a marionette with no strings.

"Hey there." The voice behind the spotlight called again and I blinked my tired eyes against the light, squinting to see who was talking to me.

"What are you doing there?"

"I used to go to school here," I said. My voice was ragged, hesitant, because I could not see the other person.

The light snapped off and I blinked again, adjusting to the sudden darkness.

"Class of '80." The voice came from inside a police

Canvas Bleeding

car. "You?"

"Class of '74," I said. It seemed like so many years had passed, like so many things had worn away at what I was, what I had dreamed of being, that I no longer had a sense of time.

"What brought you back?" he asked. He was broad-shouldered and serious, the type who had played football and been class president, gotten good grades and been liked by everyone.

I shook my head. There was nothing I could tell him.

He motioned me over to the patrol car and offered to buy me a cup of coffee. I gathered up my knapsack and climbed into the car beside him.

"Mike Morelli," he said as he stuck out a thick hand with strong fingers.

I grasped his hand firmly, shook it, and released it quickly. His touch burned in my memory, my palms sweaty and shaking. "Patrick Bates," I said.

Morelli slowly swung the patrol car out of the faculty parking lot and pointed it down the road toward the main part of town. Silence between us and the faint crackling and popping of the radio as he drove tickled at the razor-sharp edges of my nerves, rubbing the exposed ends like ground glass.

"Seventy-four," he said thoughtfully, his forehead wrinkled as if he strained to remember. "Wasn't that the year —"

"It was," I said, interrupting his question. I had wondered how long it would take him to remember.

Morelli grunted, silent again. He drove through town, down narrow streets between rows of houses washed pale by my memory of them, south to the A&W, pulling the patrol car to a halt in one of the stalls. He reached out his open window and pressed the button on the face of the speaker, ordering two coffees and a Papa Burger. He looked over at me, the

13

Michael Bracken

details of my face lost in the shadows inside the car. "You want anything else?"

"No. Coffee's fine."

"That's it, sweetheart," he said to the teenaged voice in the speaker. Then he turned to me again. "They've all left, you know."

I nodded. It wasn't hard to guess that my few remaining classmates would leave town just as I had left.

"Nobody else has ever come back," Morelli said. "Nobody I ever heard of."

I nodded again, wishing my coffee would hurry. We sat silent for a moment, watching as a Mustang careened into the parking lot, teenaged boys hanging from the open windows, yelling and waving. As soon as they saw the patrol car, they slowed and the driver carefully pulled the rusting car into a stall at the far end of the row.

"Now them boys," Morelli said, pointing his finger at the Mustang, "they don't understand what this town does."

"They will," I said. "Give them time."

Before he could respond, our coffee and his hamburger arrived. He passed a steaming cup to me, then unwrapped his hamburger and took a bite. Catsup and mustard spewed out the other side of the bun. He wiped at his uniform with a napkin, the stain already evident and too late to wipe away.

"You surprise me," Morelli finally said.

"Yes?"

"You're not what I expected." He took another bite of the hamburger, more carefully this time. "You look late sixties," he said. "Like you forgot to leave an era behind."

"Here?" I questioned. "This town's always been an era behind."

Morelli didn't know whether to laugh or take me

seriously. He considered a moment, then agreed with me. "This town moves slow. It always has."

A blonde waitress wiggled past, carrying a tray full of root beer mugs to the Mustang at the end of the aisle. Morelli's eyes followed her to the Mustang, then back into the restaurant.

"You must have a lot of bitter memories," Morelli said. "The whole class of '74 must have bitter memories."

I nodded. "It pushed them away. Kept them from coming back."

"It was a hell of an accident," he continued, oblivious to my comment. "Damn near the whole senior class." He shook his head as if to shake away the memories; then he said, "I lived three blocks away from the hotel. The explosion woke me up. My father and I watched the fire from down the street. I must have had nightmares for a month after that."

I knew what he meant. The nightmares would never end for me, had never stopped, and I didn't expect to free myself of them.

"Where were you when it happened?" Morelli asked.

"Outside," I said. "In the parking lot sneaking a drink from a bottle of Jack Daniel's. My girlfriend was inside."

"Jesus." Morelli finished his hamburger and crumpled up his napkin. "You were lucky."

"Maybe." I pulled aside my long, greasy black hair and showed him the purple splotches on the side of my face and the back of my neck. They extended far down my back and across my chest, a tattoo of burning tuxedo etched into my skin. "I went in after her. There was nothing I could do."

We sat together watching the boys in the Mustang as they piled out of the car and took their places on the hood. They laughed and swore at each other, pushed one another off the car, spilling root beer on the pavement. They were rough-and-tumble, as I had once been.

"Can I drop you someplace?" Morelli asked as he started the car. "I have to make my rounds again."

I looked over at him in the darkness of the patrol car, seeing the hard lines already forming in his young face. "I want to go back to the school." I said.

"I could take you to a motel if you want."

"The school will be fine."

He shrugged and pulled from the parking lot. "They don't know how lucky they are," Morelli said as he motioned toward the boys. "In a few years they'll realize they can't escape from this town. Nobody does," he said. "They come back sooner or later."

I listened to him ramble, watching the town crawl slowly past the car window. In ten years, nothing much had changed. D'Grasso's Hardware Store had a new coat of white paint. Henderson's Floral Shop had become Johnson's Floral Gallery. The Hi-Ho Inn had expanded into the next building. And the remains of the old hotel had been swept away, replaced by a small park in the center of town. But the Standard station where I'd had my first part-time job still had full service and the weekly newspaper still posted the front page of the most recent edition in their front window. And the houses were still the same bland blend of clapboard and vinyl siding.

"I came back," he said. "I had dreams. Big dreams. But I came back." He looked over at me. "Your class had dreams, too. But you're the first one to return."

"Most of us never had a chance to leave," I said.

"Hell of a tragedy, wasn't it? I mean, so many kids on their graduation night. They never really had a chance, did they?"

Morelli pulled the patrol car to a halt in the faculty

parking lot and I climbed out with my knapsack firmly in hand.

"You sure you don't need a ride someplace else?" he said. "I'd be happy to take you."

"No thanks," I told him. "I appreciate the offer, but I'll wait here a while."

I watched as the patrol car pulled away and I wondered if Morelli understood. Ten years is a long time for some of us.

I sat on the front porch of the school and waited, watched the moon and felt the breeze from the ocean sweep up from town to chill me. As chairman of the ten-year reunion committee, it was my responsibility to send out the invitations.

I began unpacking the knapsack; they would be arriving soon.

My classmates.

All of them.

The Seasons of Their Lives

Winter burst upon the widow Van Camp like Napalm in a sleeping village. One moment she stood on the corner of Elm and First, her arthritic legs and the cane that shook in her bony fist barely supporting her, watching little Joey Anderson sail down the street on a brand-new kick-back skateboard. The next moment she fought against a whirling dervish of snow, the tiny flakes attacking her face, her hands, and her shins, slicing her exposed skin like thousands of tiny razors. Pain had been her constant companion for nearly twenty years, so she did not cry out until she brought her hand to her face to wipe at her glasses and realized how quickly her Fall had become Winter.

"Joey!" she screamed, and the tiny daggers of snow lanced at her tongue. She didn't think him ready to witness the change of seasons. "Joey, you get home right now!"

Widow Van Camp's mouth filled with ice water when she yelled, so she sealed her thin lips against further violation. She lowered her head, planted her cane, and hobbled forward, then planted her cane a few more inches toward home. The heels of her shoes barely cleared the icy cement squares of the sidewalk and each step sent spasms of pain shooting through her arthritic legs, yet each successful step forward became a small victory in a war against the season that had threatened her for so many years.

The wind caught hold of her heavy coat, the beige one Mr. Van Camp had given her the year before Winter had taken him away, and it spun her around, threatening to topple her to the ground. She swung at the wind with her cane, cursing with every breath she fought to take, refusing to quietly enter her final season. Then she planted her cane once more, squinted through her white cat's-eye rhinestone glasses, and again aimed herself toward home.

She planted the cane and shuffled forward, her home halfway down the block a blackened silhouette momentarily visible as the storm played a child's game of peek-a-boo with her. The daggers of snow became grenades of ice, exploding shrapnel against the back of her skull and lacing through the thin wisps of blue-grey hair, her pill-box hat left home in her hurry to the store for a now-forgotten box of Orville Redenbacher's microwave popcorn.

In front of Mr. Wiliker's home, only two houses from her own, the rubber tip of her cane slid on a patch of ice, then caught on rough concrete. Off balance, she fell obliquely, feeling a rib crack as her frail body struck the sidewalk. Her cane rolled away and she scrabbled for it, her gnarled hand grasping for what she could not see, but it eluded her.

When she tried to stand without the cane, her hand

pressed firmly against the broken rib below her sagging breast, the wind slapped her down. For a moment she lay crying, inhaling water and ice and mud as she sucked air from the sidewalk. Then she reached forward, one thin arm extending until she found the crack between two cement squares. She jammed her fingers into the crack and pulled herself forward, scaling the sidewalk like a mountain climber on the face of a cliff.

Snow covered the ground quickly, smothering her when she turned her face away from the pocket of air under her chin. She reached with one hand and then the other, jamming her fingers into the sidewalk cracks and pulling herself forward inch-by-inch. Acting as the prow to her body's North Atlantic ice-breaker, her forehead scraped against the concrete and turned to a bloody pulp.

The leather buttons of her coat caught where her fingers had been and one-by-one they tore away, leaving her new wool skirt and her silk blouse exposed to the abrasion of the concrete. Each forward movement ripped a new spot open on her blouse, rubbed a new bit of her skirt bare, but she had ceased to care about her clothing.

The new sidewalk had been poured in the spring of 1974 while the entire neighborhood stood and watched, but already it pitched and bucked, the concrete squares broken by weather, upheaved by tree roots, replaced by workmen when they finally connected Mr. Wiliker to the city sewer in 1981. She drug herself past the dark spot where the youngest Gundellini boy had fallen from his Stingray while doing a wheelie, chipped a tooth and split his bottom lip wide open, spilling young blood that had never washed away; over the spot where Mr. Gundellini had pinned his oldest son to the ground, tore off the only set of love beads the town had ever seen, and shaved away shoulder-length black hair that had been the envy of all the women on the block; over the spot where Mr. Van Camp had defended the town's first Negro paper boy from the taunts and the stones of the neighborhood children; past the spot under the maple where, on a dare, Mr. Wiliker's only daughter had allowed the Gundellini boys to see her undeveloped left breast just as she was entering puberty. The maple's overhanging branches failed to stifle the snow that threatened to smother her.

She passed the Gundellinis' walk without knowing it, almost gave up half a dozen times before she reached her own, recognizable by its feel because it was the only brick walkway on the block. Silently she thanked Mr. Van Camp for his insistence almost thirty years earlier. Then she cursed him when she could no longer jam her fingers between the cracks to pull herself forward.

She forced herself to the side of the walk, grabbing and clawing at the uneven edge to pull herself toward the door of her two-bedroom bungalow, her legs trailing through the row of gladioli Mr. Wiliker had planted for her the previous summer. Still the ice knifed at the back of her exposed neck, exploded against her calves, and sent tiny rivers of ice water trailing behind her as she struggled home.

Her bloody fingers, the nails ragged and torn, pulled her forward an inch at a time. Reach, grab, and pull, the muscles in her arms screaming with pain but no worse than the pain in her side, the pain in her hip, or the pain in her calves.

She pulled herself over the one concrete step to her porch, past the wooden swing where, at 3 a.m. the morning after he'd turned fifty, Mr. Van Camp had made slow, deliberate love to her, and reached up for the door handle.

She missed the knob, but the weight of her body

Canvas Bleeding

falling against it pushed the unlatched door open and the widow Van Camp fell into her house, knocking over a walnut end table.

A 1921 tintype photo of Mr. Van Camp, decked out in his best suit, his ears protruding from under a new fedora, fell to the carpet before her. Her fingers, now claws of blood, grasped the photo and pulled it toward her breast.

The snow followed her through the open door, beating down upon her and smothering her in a thick blanket that she finally welcomed.

A moment later, little Joey Anderson stood in the widow Van Camp's doorway holding her cane, a single shaft of sunlight silhouetting his blond head. His brother's black AC/DC T-shirt hung loosely from his shoulders to his knees and a warm Spring breeze slid around his thin frame into the widow's home. He looked down at her still form, at her bloodied fingertips and scraped forehead, at her now tattered clothing. He prodded her body with the cane.

"Mom!" he screamed when the widow didn't respond, but his mother couldn't hear him from inside their three-bedroom ranch at the end of the block. "Mom!"

Mr. Wiliker, publisher of the town's weekly newspaper since his retirement from the Marines in 1947, and the widow Van Camp's only suitor since Mr. Van Camp's death, heard Joey's screams and came running from his house and across the Gundellinis' lawn, the unraked fall leaves spraying to either side as his size eleven wingtips kicked them away.

Little Joey Anderson watched silently as the snow abandoned the widow Van Camp and caught Mr. Wiliker unprepared, driving him cursing and screaming to the ground.

His mother had once explained the seasons of their

Michael Bracken

lives, but little Joey Anderson — still enjoying his own Spring — had never before seen Winter. He watched, fascinated, until Mr. Wiliker stopped screaming and the snow he had yet to see but had just begun to comprehend disappeared in the summer heat.

Dead Air Days

*T*riple-digit dry heat, no breeze. I leaned against a barren pecan tree and watched the horizon shimmer, heat waves rising off the parched ground. A train whistled two miles off and in the heat I saw my father's ghosts.

I wore a sweat-stained gimme cap, a long-billed baseball hat emblazoned with the logo of a now-defunct granary. I'd tucked my kerchief under the back of the cap, letting it hang over my neck where sweat glued it to my skin. A brand new green-and-gold T-shirt clung to my chest and back, half-moons of sweat darkening my underarms. I wore it tucked into a tight-fitting pair of faded Levi's and my battered Ropers — low-heeled cowboy boots — had long ago molded themselves to the shapes of my feet.

My father had once sat in this same spot, a deer rifle cradled in his hands, the butt of the rifle slamming

Michael Bracken

against his shoulder each time he squeezed the trigger.

"I got three, maybe four of them myself," he'd told me once. I'd just turned twelve, the same age he'd been, and we were in the barn changing the oil in his '59 Chevrolet Apache. "They came running at us, a whole line of them, men, women, and children. We just picked them off like ducks at the shooting gallery."

The Apache sat twenty or thirty feet behind me now, too far away for me to return to the cooler of Lone Star I'd left in the bed. I opened the one bottle I'd carried up the rise with me and took a quick swallow.

That afternoon in the barn, my father lifted the tooled leather patch from his left eye, showing me the blind orb beneath. "Everything ended when Sammy Ledbetter's Winchester kicked out a hot shell."

Ledbetter had been standing to my father's left, sighting down the v-notch of his rifle and taking down two for every one of my father's.

"Kept me out of the war, though," my father said as he fitted the patch back into place. "Got to be grateful for that."

I squinted against the harsh midday sun, counting the first dozen coming into view.

"I still see them, sometimes," my father said years later, after mother had passed and we found ourselves alone in the kitchen with a six pack of Lone Star and a window air conditioner that struggled in vain to push tepid air around the room. "On dead air days like today."

They could have been farm workers or college professors and it wouldn't have made any difference to the men gathered that day. During the Great Depression, Immigration officials packed more than 400,000 men, women, and children into sealed boxcars and shipped them southward toward the border, leaving behind whatever possessions they could not carry.

Dust storms had destroyed crops throughout the Midwest and god-fearing Christian farmers now lived in the shanties and worked the fields they had once willingly relinquished to brown-skinned foreigners.

The men with my father had each paid twenty dollars to stand on the rise by the pecan tree, money that had been passed from Postmaster Wilson to a pair of Immigration officials riding with the train.

"I had my first beer that day," my father explained. "Woody brought a washtub filled with ice and beer and your granddad pulled one out for each of us. I can still see the flecks of ice glittering on the bottles and the water dripping from his hand."

My father drank that first beer, foam sliding down his chin and his chest, and he'd mopped his forehead with an old undershirt, waiting and listening to granddad and the other men laugh at jokes he'd been too young to understand.

"Smitty spotted the first one rising from the heat," my father explained. "Your granddad sat me down against the tree and told me not to fire until the others started. It seemed like we waited a long time."

My father passed two summers ago and we laid him to rest up in Crawfordsville, next to mother. After Sammy Ledbetter's errant shell had half-blinded my father, granddad had not returned to the shoot. A few years later the United States entered World War II and the men who weren't drafted were no longer available.

Three days after we buried my father, the temperature soared to 112 and heat rose from the ground in waves. I'd been in the back field repairing a break in the fence when I thought I saw someone approaching from over the horizon. I straightened and lifted my hat, mopping my forehead with the back of my arm. Just as I lifted my hand to wave to the oncoming stranger, he dropped from view.

Michael Bracken

I blinked against the heat, scanning the horizon to see where he'd gone. When the stranger didn't reappear, I returned to the task at hand not realizing I'd seen one of my father's ghosts until much, much later.

My father had been the last man alive who'd participated in the events that day, the only one who apparently ever spoke of it, and he'd passed the memory to me.

"I was sitting here," he said after we trudged to the top of the rise the summer before I turned thirty-nine. He showed me where each of the men had been standing or sitting that day. "Your granddad was back here, behind me to the right. Over there, Smitty, and next to him was Mr. Johnson and Woody stood next to the washtub of beer. Sammy Ledbetter stood here, to my left, and on the other side of him were Postmaster Wilson and Harley Pitzer, eight years before we sent him to Congress."

My father pointed to the horizon. "The train stopped two miles west of here. It must have been about one o'clock because we'd had lunch at the house before driving out. They opened up a couple of the box cars and herded them people into the scrub toward us."

My father turned his back on the memory and stood facing me. He had crumpled in on himself over the years and he leaned heavily on an aluminum walker. His skin had grown as dark and leathery as his eye patch and thin wisps of white hair lay across the top of his nearly-bald pate.

"Afterward, Harley and Smitty walked into the scrub and kicked over the bodies. I heard three more shots before your granddad bundled me into the Ford and carried me to the doctor. Hunting accident, he told the doctor and that's all that was ever said about it."

I took another swallow of beer and squinted against the midday sun, wishing I'd remembered my sunglasses.

A week before his death, my father called out my name from his hospital bed. He'd been blind for nearly a year by then and he couldn't see that I sat only a few feet away. I rose from the chair and took his hand.

"They're coming for me," he whispered hoarsely. "I can see them coming over the horizon, rising from the heat. They've taken all the others."

He coughed, and his entire body shook. Then he called out for granddad and for the next three days nothing he said made sense to anyone but me. The killing fields had never been discovered, the dead never reported as missing, and not one of the participants had ever revealed the things they had done.

Yet, the sins of my father became mine. I remembered details of what he had told me so well that I could see the entire day unfold around me. I took one last swallow of warm beer from the open bottle between my legs, wiped the palms of my hands on the thighs of my Levi's, then slid my father's deer rifle from its padded case.

I raised the rifle to my shoulder and took careful aim at the dead Mexicans swarming the horizon.

In the Death Ward

*I*t would be difficult to describe what they did as making love since they didn't love each other and never had. What happened was an act of raw animalistic sex — the merging of two separate beings into one for a brief period of time that left them both flushed and covered with a sheen of perspiration, struggling for breath, and still entwined in a pool of their sexual juices ten minutes after they'd finished.

Less than three miles away, Angela's husband clung to life with the grim determination of a career Marine executing his last mission and Donald's wife of twelve years had become little more than the biological extension of nearly a million dollars worth of life support equipment.

As they drifted into sleep on the king-sized Motel 6 bed they'd shared so many times before, their room momentarily lit up with a red strobe. Yet another

Michael Bracken

ambulance screamed down the highway toward the hospital, a metallic angel of mercy on steel-belted wings battling the odds at ninety-one miles per hour. Angela, always more sensitive to the ambient sounds of impending death, stirred, rolling onto her stomach with a groan before settling into her new position.

A mutual desire for the last square of apple crisp in the hospital cafeteria months earlier had bound them to one another; repeated visits to the intensive care ward had twisted the strands of their lives together until they could no longer be separated, sustaining one another like incestuous vampires of pain and suffering feeding in a daisy-chain of mutual need and desire.

"She could live for many years," Donald told Angela over twin Styrofoam cups of cold coffee one evening after he'd spent the entire day holding his wife's hand and telling her of his latest accomplishments at the computer repair center where he worked. "There's brain activity."

"He doesn't recognize me," Angela explained one morning after she'd cradled her husband's head in her lap for three straight hours, her dress ultimately stained by his tears. "The chemotherapy failed. They only gave him a few months to live but he won't admit defeat."

After emptying a bottle of Johnny Walker Red a few weeks later, they'd discovered the economical and emotional benefits of a single motel room. Under other circumstances they would not have found one another attractive — nearly twenty years separated them and the war he'd fled to Canada to avoid had taken her only son and threatened to take her husband — yet the intense merging of one body into the other, the physical feedback loop of shared pain sucked them dry and replenished them as nothing else could.

Just after three a.m. Angela awoke screaming.

Donald sat up and gathered her into his arms, muffling her scream with his shoulder. He rocked her back and forth, feeling her breasts slapping gently against his chest. Then he brushed her limp grey hair away from her face with his thick fingers and kissed the tears away from the folds of skin around her eyes.

"He's gone," she cried.

As if to confirm her nightmare, the phone rang, its shrill electronic chirping more irritating at that moment than any other sound in the world. Donald answered, said, "She'll be there in a few minutes," and hung up.

They dressed, pulling on the same clothes they'd worn the previous day — Angela in the simple flower-patterned shift she'd made for herself two summers previous, Donald in his tight-fitting faded blue jeans and his Chicago Bears jersey.

When they arrived at the hospital, they smelled of sleep, and sweat, and sex, their odor stronger even than the antiseptic hospital smell that pervaded everything else.

Donald watched Angela disappear into an office, guided by a gaunt young doctor whose thin fingers had clamped onto Angela's elbow the moment she'd arrived. She didn't even glance back toward him, her own grief so all-consuming.

Donald slipped into his wife's room a moment later when he thought the overworked night nurses weren't paying attention and he pulled a chair up next to her bed. At first, he simply held his wife's hand, only gradually realizing that sometime during the night her brain waves had flatlined. Ever the innocent victim of others' misfortunes, the last spark of his wife had been extinguished by a breeze from the hem of Death's robe as he'd strode boldly down the hall to do final battle with Angela's husband.

Donald had spent nearly every day since the motor-

Michael Bracken

cycle accident sitting beside his wife and teaching himself how her life support equipment functioned. He'd prepared himself for this day so he could keep the promise he'd once made to her.

Still holding his wife's hand in one of his own, Donald reached out and began shutting down her mechanical extensions. Within moments, alarms sounded at the nurses' station, but Donald refused to move from his wife's side when the nurses began streaming into the room.

The crash cart arrived too late.

Donald and Angela saw each other again a few hours later when the police finally arrived to question Donald. She stood at the end of the hall, the hem of her dress bunched into one gnarled fist. He stared over his shoulder at her as a burly uniformed officer guided him into an empty room, but they no longer knew one another.

Outside the hospital the thin wail of an ambulance siren ground to a halt but the red lights continued to strobe into the room where Donald began to answer questions.

Their daisy chain had broken while elsewhere in the death ward another waited to be forged.

Mermaid

*E*ddie Waterford burped. The taste of stale beer erupted in his mouth and he tried to spit it out.

Above him a single gull cried. Eddie squinted against the morning sun as he searched the sky. When he couldn't find the gull, Eddie continued walking northward along the beach. His sport jacket hung limply from his left hand, the checkered sleeves dragging through the sand.

He burped again. He'd drank too much the night before and his memories of the evening had disintegrated. He'd awoken on the beach, his jacket covered with vomit and wet sand, his silk tie wrapped around the bloody knuckles of his right fist. From the pain, Eddie suspected his nose was broken.

As soon as he'd been able to stand, Eddie began walking north, picking the direction without thinking. Now, his footprints and the track of his sport coat strung behind him for nearly two miles.

Ahead he saw a woman laying at the water's edge. He was beside her before he realized she was dead.

Michael Bracken

Eddie dropped his jacket, then bent down beside the body. She lay on her back, staring up at the morning sun. Her long blonde hair splayed around her face, a wet evening dress clung to her firm body. Her lips were parted slightly. Neither bloated nor broken, she was a woman more beautiful in death than any he'd known in life. Eddie stared into her eyes, then reached out to touch her.

And, as his fingers touched her cheek, he felt her pain. The pain of her divorce, the murder of her only child, the eroding of her ability to cope with the world around her. And he felt something else: the release of her pain as the ocean swelled around her, the serenity she now felt.

Eddie stared out at the horizon, seeing only ocean until finally it met the sky. He sat in the sand beside her, holding her hand in his, and heard her calling to him, calling to him like no woman ever had.

The ocean licked at the beach, sending foam tendrils up the sand toward them as Eddie stood, kicked off his shoes, and waded into the cold water. He began to swim, the tide pulling him away from the beach, the salt water stinging his open wounds.

He swam without looking back.

Karl and the Shadow Box

The shop was cluttered with half-finished doll houses, each filled with miniature furniture and fixtures. Shadow boxes lining the walls were crammed with tiny beds, dressers, sofas, chairs, lamps, throw rugs, desks, sinks, record albums, coat racks, paintings, and all manner of household goods.

Karl stood at the front counter which, save for the chair behind it, was the only full-sized furniture in the shop. He looked at the young woman behind the counter. She was shorter than he, with dark hair cascading down her shoulders.

"Do you have a miniature ice cream cone?" he asked.

"Yes," she replied. "We have everything."

"Fantastic." He'd been in four different doll shops that afternoon before crossing the river into southern Illinois to visit a shop he'd never been to.

"What flavor?" she asked.

Michael Bracken

"Mint chocolate chip." He thought she was kidding, and answered with his favorite flavor. "In a sugar cone."

She led him through the shop. Dust motes hung in the damp air and tickled his nostrils when he inhaled. Tall stacks of unopened doll house kits threatened to topple over as he brushed past them. She stopped in a store room. It, like the displays, was a cluttered collection of things.

"We haven't put these out yet," she said. She reached into a half-opened cardboard box. A moment later she pulled her hand free. In her fingers she clutched a tiny ice cream cone: mint chocolate chip in a sugar cone. It was a perfect reproduction — exactly what Karl needed to finished his latest shadow box.

They returned to the front of the shop. She stood behind the counter, turned slightly to watch two boys playing outside.

The setting sun shone through the flimsy material of her white blouse and Karl could see her breasts silhouetted against the light. They were sagging slightly under their own weight: she wasn't wearing a bra.

Karl cleared his throat. "How much?"

"What?" The girl returned her attention to him.

He held up the ice cream cone. "How much?"

"Take it," she said with a smile. "We've got more."

"But . . ." Karl started. Then he shrugged and dropped the tiny cone into his shirt pocket. He shook his head slightly in wonder.

Before he closed the door on his way out, she said, "Remember us next time. We have everything."

*I*t took Karl more than an hour to drive back to his

Canvas Bleeding

St. Louis apartment. He sat at his kitchen table and carefully mounted the ice cream cone to the plate on the table in his shadow box. Then he sat back and looked at it.

Although Karl had never captured people in his shadow boxes, they evoked a feeling of having just been deserted by various members of the families he imagined living within his tiny rooms. The old-fashioned kitchen captured in the shadow box before him had been host to a small child who'd been momentarily called out of the room, but who would return quickly to finished his ice cream cone.

It had taken months to collect and assemble all the tiny pieces of furniture necessary to construct the kitchen in his shadow box but, within a few hours, Karl placed the shadow box in the closet with all the others he'd assembled. He'd shown them to no one, and no one but the manager ever visited his grimy second floor apartment.

"*I* need a box of Quaker Oats."

"Instant?" she asked.

"No," Karl said. "The old-fashioned round box."

He had been to all the St. Louis shops. As before, none had carried just what he was looking for. He'd lived in St. Louis all his life, but until he'd come searching for the more off-beat accouterments necessary for constructing his shadow boxes, Karl had never crossed the river into Illinois.

She led him back through the towering displays of stoves, refrigerators, and kitchen tables. She led him past the disorganized displays of toilets, bathtubs, and sinks. Finally, she stopped before a dusty display case.

39

Michael Bracken

She climbed on an old crate, lightly steadying herself with her fingertips on his shoulders, and reached into a small crevice between a Victorian living room and a Pop Art bedroom.

She handed him the Quaker Oats box and climbed down. "Is that all you need?"

He nodded. "But I'd like to look around for a while."

"Sure." She returned to the chair between the counter and the front window. Karl watched her adjust the chair before sitting. Then he walked slowly around the shop, peering into the display cases, carefully avoiding the unstable stacks of boxes littering the floor. He looked at the shelves stretching ten feet up to the water-stained ceiling of the old building. And every so often, Karl stole a glance at the young woman, still sitting on her chair.

Her slender figure was clad in a pair of tight-fitting jeans, slightly worn, but not worn out, and a loose, diaphanous blouse. She wore no make-up, and didn't need any. Her dark skin hinted at a Mediterranean influence, but her other features were less revealing — there was no Roman nose or English chin to belie her heritage.

Karl wandered back to the counter. "You're not in the phone book."

She turned to him. "We don't need to be. People who need us, find us."

He held up the tiny Quaker Oats box.

"It's yours," she said. "We have others."

"I can't do that." Karl pulled a dollar from his wallet. She didn't reach for the bill, so he let it drop to the counter top.

She smiled at him as he left.

Canvas Bleeding

*I*t was hot in Karl's apartment. His window air-conditioner had broken again and he couldn't afford to replace it. Angry that he was unable to repair it this time, Karl stalked down the street to the tavern on the corner. It was a dismal place, like most of the neighborhood, but it was cool inside and the hamburgers were as greasy as the fries were plentiful. He ordered dinner and a beer.

When he'd finished the burger and fries, Karl ordered a second beer. He dropped a pinch of salt into the glass mug and sipped at the cheap off-brand. An incomplete shadow box was waiting for him on his kitchen table, the oak paneling and the dark shag carpet waiting for the hand-built shelves to be attached to the back wall. Store-purchased furniture waited on the kitchen table.

*I*t was his third visit in as many months. This time Karl didn't bother stopping at the other shops first.

"How about a quill pen and a jar of ink for a roll-top desk?"

This time she didn't answer him, but walked a few steps from her counter, reached into a dusty shadow box, and pulled out just what he'd been imagining.

Karl was sorry she didn't have to search through the back of the shop to find his trinket. He liked following her through the dank and dusty doll shop. He liked the delicate smell of her perfume as it wafted behind her.

Today her hair was tied back in a loose pony tail. Otherwise, she looked the same as she had before.

It was warm in the shop, and the heat and his sweat

Michael Bracken

were causing him to itch under his closely cropped beard. He scratched lightly at his cheeks. He didn't want to leave.

"How long have you worked here?" he asked.

"Forever." She laughed. "It sure seems that way."

"Do many people come in here?" He'd never run into other customers.

"A few. They keep me going." She brushed a loose strand of dark hair away from her face.

Karl had run out of conversation and felt himself beginning to flush. He pulled a five dollar bill from his wallet and dropped it on the glass counter top. She didn't pick it up and she didn't offer change. Karl didn't expect any.

*I*t was dark when Karl returned home. He flipped on the living room light as he entered the little apartment, placed the pen and ink set carefully on the end table, and flopped onto the couch. A light cloud of dust billowed from the cushions.

He was tired. The drive home had taken much longer than he had expected: the Cardinals were playing a home game and traffic on the Poplar Street Bridge had been backed up into East St. Louis, Illinois.

Karl fell asleep on the couch, dreams of the girl in the doll shop causing him to toss and turn. His last girlfriend had dumped him while they were still in high school, and he'd never dated anyone twice since then. The employees at most doll shops were pimply-faced teenagers, so Karl never had the opportunity to be come acquainted with anyone at his usual haunts.

When he awoke, sunlight was streaming into his dark eyes. He groused as he sat up. He hadn't expected to spend the night on the couch. He pulled off his tattered tennis shoes and sweat-soaked socks. He dug his toes into the dirty carpeting, stretched, and made his way to the shower.

The cool water relaxed his cramped muscles and tickled the hair on his chest. The shampoo lathered into great gobs of foam as he scrubbed his hair.

It had been three days since his last shower. He had to take better care of himself.

*E*ach month a check from a trust fund arrived at his apartment. If he was willing to live frugally, Karl had no need to hold down a job. Karl was careful with his monthly allotment, allowing only the joys of assembling shadow boxes to dip into his savings.

A week had passed since his last visit to the doll shop and, with the most recent check padding his checking account and vague ideas about his next shadow box already forming in the back of his mind, he headed across the river.

She was sitting behind the counter when he drove up. He stopped his battered Chevy in front of the doll shop, climbed out, and strode slowly up the two concrete steps to the door. He smiled at her when he stepped through the doorway. She returned his greeting.

"What can I do for you today?" she asked.

"I'm not sure," he said. "I'm not sure what I want to do next."

"Look around. Get some ideas."

Karl had planned on doing just that. He wandered through the stacks of furniture and displays. Ultimately, though, he wound his way back to the front counter.

"Do you live near here?" he asked.

"I have a few rooms upstairs," she said. "It isn't much, but I'm happy. How about you?"

"St. Louis."

"It's a long drive isn't it?"

"It's not bad," he said. "After all, you have —"

"— everything," she finished.

"Everything," he agreed.

She smiled at him, lips parting slightly to reveal just the tips of her teeth. She hadn't noticed, but a button had come undone on her blouse, and when she turned just so, Karl could peek in and see the white mounds of her breasts and the rosy red of her nipples as they rubbed against her blouse.

"Have you found anything yet?"

"A shadow box." It was long and narrow, an odd shape for a shadow box, and he'd found it deep in the bowels of the doll shop.

She looked at it as he placed it on the counter. "How long have you been doing this?"

"Five or six years," Karl said. "I started with model cars when I was a kid and changed over when I grew older. I think I'm trying to recapture a piece of my past."

She nodded.

"What are you asking for this?" He was reaching for his wallet.

"Make me something pretty in it," she said.

Karl nodded and let his wallet slide back into place.

"Maybe next time you come over, you could bring me one of your finished boxes. . . ."

Karl brightened. "Maybe I will."

He stood at the counter a few moments, realized he had nothing else to say, and made his way to the door. Just before he stepped outside, he turned back to her and said, "By the way, my name's Karl."

*H*e sat at his kitchen table, a half-eaten tuna sandwich on the plate beside him, a now-warm glass of cola by his right elbow. Carefully he painted the interior of the shadow box. Mixing the proper color had been difficult — he'd wanted just the right shade of brown.

He coughed into his fist and leaned back against the yellow plastic kitchen chair. This would be the ultimate test of his abilities: he was trying to duplicate an existing room.

"*I* brought you this," Karl said to the girl a few days later. He placed a shadow box on the counter. It was the kitchen that had brought him to the shop the first time.

She examined it carefully. "It's beautifully done," she said. "It's better than the other shadow boxes people bring in here."

"Thank you." Karl's blush was hidden behind his neatly trimmed beard. He'd never shown a completed shadow box to anyone before.

She picked it up, turned, and placed it in the front window. Outside, dark clouds gathered for a storm. "I want everybody to see what can be done," she said.

Karl watched her. She didn't seem to change much; her style of dress hadn't altered since he'd first visited the shop.

"Need anything special today?" She brushed her hair away from her face.

Karl listed a few items and she led him to them. He

needed more paint, a new brush, some faded wallpaper, and miscellaneous supplies. The miniature miniatures he'd have to make himself — or so he thought until she led him past a display he'd never seen before. He paused to stare at the miniature doll house and the extra-tiny accessories designed to accompany it. He picked a few items from the display.

As they returned to the front counter, the storm broke loose. The street lights blinked on in the darkness, then winked off when lightning streaked across the sky. Hail pelted the window, rattling against the glass.

"Looks nasty, doesn't it?"

Karl nodded. "I'll have to get home before it gets any worse. The weatherman's predicted high winds and severe thunderstorms."

"Why don't you stay here tonight?" She paused for a heartbeat. "It looks too nasty to drive."

He looked out the window, then at her. "If it's okay...."

She locked the front door and led him to a stairway in back.

A divider separated her one large room into two. She fixed cold cut sandwiches at the kitchen counter and they ate them sitting cross-legged on her four-poster bed watching old reruns.

"Turn around, Karl," she said after he'd turned the TV off. She had unbuttoned her blouse. Slowly, tentatively, Karl reached out to touch one of her hardening nipples.

"It's okay," she whispered. She took his hand and held it against her breast, then pulled him slowly across her as she lay back against the pillows.

*D*etermined to finish the shadow box before he returned to the doll shop, Karl worked long hours the next few days. It would be a gift for her, and it was as perfect as Karl could make it.

*H*e drove slowly into the small town and parked his car in its usual place. Then he realized: the doll shop was gone. A few scraggly patches of grass covered the lot where the shop had been.

He stared up and down the street, counting the buildings, reading the signs, convincing himself that the empty lot before him had been the site of the doll shop.

Then he hurried into the store next door: a leathercraft shop tended by a leftover from the sixties.

"Where's the doll shop?" Karl asked.

The long-haired man behind the counter looked up at him. "The what?"

"What happened to the doll shop next door?"

"That ain't a doll shop, man, that's a real estate office."

"No. On the other side."

The man laughed at him. "That's been an empty lot as long as I've been here," he said. "You feel okay?"

"Yeah. Sure." Karl stumbled out the door to his car. He pulled the new shadow box from the front seat to convince himself of what the shop looked like. There it was, just as his memory had pictured it: perfect in every detail.

Michael Bracken

He stared at the empty lot for a long time before he realized. Perfect in every detail.

Karl looked at the shadow box again. There was the girl, seated behind the counter, wearing her tight jeans and loose white blouse, all just the same as he remembered.

"We have everything," she'd told him.

Now Karl held everything in his hands.

The Passenger

I towed the battered red 1959 Corvette home on a trailer behind my pickup, smiling and constantly taking quick peeks in the rearview mirror to remind myself that I wasn't dreaming. Even though I had drained my savings account to buy the car, I knew I had paid less than the car was worth. Jack Carlson's widow had been anxious to rid herself of the car Jack had died in and, despite my qualms about buying a car that had been involved in the death of someone I knew, I recognized a bargain when it fell into my lap. After all, the car had sustained only minor damage in the wreck: the dual headlights on the driver's side had shattered and the front bumper was badly dented. The paint job had taken a beating and I was sure a half-dozen other things would surface when I began work on it. Still, I didn't expect any problems repairing the car.

Michael Bracken

I was still smiling when I pulled into the driveway at home. Stopping before the garage, I climbed out and opened one of the large double-doors. Inside the garage I already had a mint-condition Stingray and a workshop ready to begin renovation of my latest find. Over the years I had reconditioned almost two dozen muscle cars on my own time, mostly working for friends, but Corvettes had always been my favorite car and I was always on the lookout for a damaged 'Vette at a good price.

I backed the trailer up to the open garage door, then I pushed the Corvette off the trailer into its appointed space. After parking the truck and removing the trailer, I went into the house for a cold bottle of soda and a handful of pretzels.

Returning to the garage with my snack, I pulled on a pair of greasy overalls and opened the Corvette's hood. Two hours later, the car up on blocks, my snack devoured, I lay underneath examining the transmission housing. As I lay there I got the prickly feeling on the back of my neck like when I was being watched. I pushed myself out from under the car and stood up. When I looked around the garage I found that I was alone. I stared out through the open garage doors, seeing only the neighbor's dog crossing my yard, and shrugged. My visitor, if I'd had one, had disappeared.

I wiped my hands on a rag and slid back under the car.

*T*he feeling returned sporadically during the next month while I worked on the Corvette, but I shook it off. Spending all of my free time in the garage with the car made me a bit edgy.

Canvas Bleeding

Finally, though, the Corvette sat purring in the driveway, awaiting its first official test drive. I walked around it once, admiring the nine-spoke grill and the Polo White coves accented against the Sportsman Red body. After one slow trip around the car, I slid into the driver's seat, feeling the powerful car idling under me. Then I reached down to the T-handle shifter and slipped the 'Vette into gear.

I drove easily out of my driveway and down the street to the first stop sign, then left towards the old mill road. I put the car through its paces, testing the brakes and the acceleration a half dozen times before I brought the car up to a comfortable cruising speed. Together, we sailed down miles of flat and featureless highway, slowly winding our way deeper into southern Illinois.

I was almost to O'Shea when a glimpse of something caught the corner of my eye and I turned to look at the passenger seat. It was empty, as I'd expected it to be, but I couldn't shake the feeling that I'd seen someone sitting beside me.

Reaching for the radio, I spun the dial across a dozen stations before I found one playing the right kind of driving music: rockabilly and country with a solid beat. I drummed my palms against the steering wheel, keeping time with the music and forcing out all stray thoughts.

In O'Shea, I stopped at a Burgerbarn for a double Barnburger, large fries, and a cola. While sitting in one of the customer corrals, I stared through the plate glass window at the '59 Corvette. I was proud of all the work I'd done to restore the car to its full glory.

When I left the fast-food restaurant, I slid back into the Corvette, tucked the half-finished cola between my thighs, and started the car. It still purred as softly as it had at home. I shifted the car into gear and pointed

Michael Bracken

the Corvette back out the old mill road toward home.

As I left O'Shea, the feeling of being watched returned but was forgotten a few miles later when the accelerator stuck. The Corvette began gaining speed. I kicked at the accelerator pedal and felt no response. I slammed my foot on the brake. The pedal was mushy and sank to the floorboard without effect.

The speedometer needle had crept up over 70.

With my left foot I stomped the clutch to the floor. I grabbed the T-handle shifter and dropped the car into neutral. I could hear the engine whine under the hood as it continued accelerating.

The highway ahead of me was flat and empty so I kept the Corvette pointed dead-ahead. The car freewheeled and the speedometer slowly crept downward. I reached for the ignition key, turned the engine off, and continued coasting along the road.

When I finally pulled the car onto the shoulder of the two-lane highway, I climbed out and opened the hood. I saw nothing out of place. Getting back in the car, I tested the accelerator and the brakes. They felt fine so I carefully restarted the engine.

I dropped the car into gear, took my foot off the brake, and eased forward. Then I slammed the brake again, almost throwing myself into the steering wheel. Convinced that everything was back in working order, I pulled onto the highway.

When I felt the presence again I didn't turn my head. Instead I concentrated on looking from the corner of my right eye, slowly adjusting to the straining angle. I could see someone sitting in the passenger seat: a young brunette with dark hair spilling in waves of silkiness down to her gently rounded shoulders. She was simply dressed, wearing a pair of slacks and a tight white sweater that accented the gentle curves of her young body. She seemed to be in her early 20s and she was staring out the windshield of the car.

As I watched, her sweater slowly turned crimson with blood.

I gagged and jerked my eyes back to the thin asphalt thread stretching ahead of me. When I looked back, my passenger was gone.

I shook my head again, trying to clear away the horrifying image that still lingered there, then I turned up the radio and tuned in a hard rock station that guaranteed to drive away any thought with the heavy, pounding beat and the screaming guitars.

When I returned home, I sat at the kitchen table for a few minutes, trying to pull myself together. Then I picked up the wall phone and dialed the number of Carlson's widow. When she answered, I identified myself and asked, "What happened to Jack in the Corvette?"

"What do you mean?" she answered. She sounded as if she wanted to hide something from me.

"How did Jack die?" I asked. "He wasn't drinking. I know Jack didn't drink."

"I don't know," she told me, her voice cracking. "I don't know anything about it. I just know what Jack told me."

"What did he tell you?" I demanded.

"Nothing," she said, uncertainly. "Just that... well, he said he felt nervous when he drove the Corvette."

"Nervous. How?"

"I don't know. I really don't. Can't you just leave me alone? Jack's gone now. He's dead."

I could tell that she was still grieving for Jack, but I had to know more about the car. I asked again.

"He just had a wreck," she said. "Just like the guy

Michael Bracken

that owned it before him. He was driving on the bluff highway and he had a wreck."

She seemed to break down then, unable to control herself. I politely told her good-bye. Just before I hung up, I heard her voice again. "The car killed him," she said. "The car killed all of them."

I saw my passenger again a week later. She was sitting in the Corvette beside me, not moving, her eyes straining to see something far ahead of us on the road. I reached up slowly and adjusted the dash-mounted rear-view mirror until I could see her reflection.

"Who are you?" I demanded.

She didn't answer.

"What are you doing here?"

She didn't move.

"What do you want from me?"

Still no response.

Angry, I turned toward her.

She was gone. The seat was empty.

Cold sweat seeped through my pores. I mopped at my brow with the back of my hand, driving beads of sweat down into my eyes, stinging them. I blinked the sweat away.

After turning the car around, I drove straight home. When I got into the house I called Bobby and canceled out of the early evening football game. When he asked, I honestly told him I wasn't feeling well.

I sat in the kitchen for a long time after that, staring through the living room and out the bay window at the red and white Corvette parked in the driveway. Finally the lure was too strong, the curiosity outweighing the fear I had.

I returned to the car.

The sun had begun sinking in the west, sending streaks of orange and red fire across the pale blue evening sky. I carefully considered the Corvette, then I slid into the driver's seat.

"Okay," I said aloud. "If you want me, here I am."

Then I started the car, dropped it into gear, and backed out of the driveway. I drove in no particular direction, turning at random, following no preconceived route. By the time the sun finally disappeared I found myself following the winding curve of the river on the bluff highway, the same road where Carlson had died.

I accelerated, surpassing the speed limit as the cool summer breeze whipped over and around the windshield, sending my hair streaming back toward the seat.

Before long I saw her there. She was sitting still, straining to watch the road ahead, squinting against the darkness and the twin beams of light knifing through the night.

I had half my attention on her, trying to watch her to see what she would do. I had driven the bluff highway so many times I felt I could drive it blindfolded, but I wasn't prepared when my passenger raised her arm and pointed out the 'Vette's windshield.

It was the first movement she'd ever made and I swung my attention fully toward her. She stayed solid for a moment, like I could reach out and touch her, then she disappeared.

Then I swung my attention to the road ahead of me. Caught in the twin beams of light stood a woman, her arm thrown up to shield her eyes from the blinding light that had her trapped against the darkness. She was pointing toward me. Beside her lay a small boy.

Something was wrong. They weren't moving.

I spun the wheel of the Corvette, fighting with it as

the car crossed the median into the oncoming lanes. From out of the darkness a semi appeared, coming straight for me.

I spun the wheel back, trying to wrestle the car under my control. I saw that the woman in the white sweater and the boy still hadn't moved. And I saw why: the boy's leg was twisted under him at an unnatural angle. Blood seemed to pool around his leg.

I fought the wheel, and continued fighting it. I didn't have many choices and in that tiny moment I realized what Carlson had done. He had seen the woman in the road and had realized who she was. He'd turned onto the shoulder, though, finally bringing the car to a halt against some solid object in order to avoid the mother and child.

Unable to stop the car, I sought the same conclusion Carlson had, but I didn't have quite the same choice. The 'Vette was pointed at the barrier on the river side of the road.

I stomped on the accelerator and at the last minute I pushed my door open and rolled free of the car, landing on the rough gravel of the shoulder and sliding to a halt.

The Corvette struck the guard rail, went straight through it, and tumbled end over end down the steep bluff toward the river. It exploded before it struck the rushing water.

I lay in the gravel on the shoulder of the road and watched the 'Vette disintegrate, wondering how many other people had owned the car since her death and if any others had walked away from it. As the last flame died away I knew there would be nothing left of the car to salvage; there would be nothing left to haunt.

When I finally looked back across the road, it was empty. The semi had disappeared and the mother and child were gone. My hands bloody and bruised, I pushed myself to my feet and limped across the highway to search for the place where they had been.

I never found it. I realized then that the loss of the Corvette was nothing compared to the torment she had been through, of the lives that had been lost because of it.

As dawn peeked over the horizon, I began the long walk home.

Fine Print

Charlie Walker rubbed the worn wood of the bar as he drank, watching the dust motes dance in the sliver of sunlight that stole in through a gap in the heavy curtains. The summer sun was a rubicund ball of fire sliding from the evening sky, sending its last rays of the day to dance across the rows of bottles lining the wall behind the bar.

He watched as his reflection in the bar mirror took another drink from the tumbler and tried to straighten his tie. Over his reflection's shoulder, Charlie could see the rest of the room behind him. It was hidden in shadows, each booth a cavern of darkness. He thought he could see the silhouettes of people in the booths, talking and gesturing and laying across the tables, but when he turned to look over his shoulder they were gone again, lost in the depths of the shadows.

He wiped at his eyes, silently cursed the drink in his hand, and ordered another. The shadows cast deceptive reflections in the mirror and he couldn't focus clearly on them.

Michael Bracken

"The stock market's down again," the bartender said, motioning to the day-old *Wall Street Journal* at Charlie's elbow.

"It'll bounce back soon enough. It always does." Charlie covered the paper with his arm. He had been forced to let his subscription expire, and he lived from day to day on the discarded copies of his condominium neighbors. He didn't want the bartender to see the paper's date.

"You in the market?" The bartender was a thin, hawk-nosed man wearing a dirty white shirt and a stained apron. Charlie looked at the man's face for the hundredth time, but was still unable to guess at his age.

"I used to be. Used to be pretty good at handling my money."

"What happened?" The bartender stood in front of Charlie, idly polishing the dark wood of the bar with the corner of his apron.

"Bad investments. It was a go-go market there for a while, and it went-went all right. Took my money with it."

"It's a lot like horse racing."

"I don't gamble," Charlie said.

"You put all your hopes on a company, or a horse, and you either win, lose, or draw. Horses are much faster, though. You don't spend a year watching the little numbers in the paper as your stock goes up and down. You put your money down at the window, and half an hour later the race is over. It makes more sense."

Charlie smiled to himself: the bartender didn't know what he was talking about.

The sliver of sunlight had finally disappeared, and the dim yellow lights of the bar were barely holding their own against the darkness. The atmosphere had changed very little, though. No one had come in since Charlie, and no one had left. He could hear the buzz of conversation coming from the booths behind him, but, like the reflections in the mirror, he could separate none of the words from their background, and when he tried to concentrate on any thread of conversation, it disappeared into the shadows of white noise.

"What about contests?" the bartender asked. He was still standing opposite Charlie. "You seem like a man willing to take a chance. You ever get involved in contests?"

"One or two. Not often." Charlie looked up at the bartender. "Why?"

"I'm a judge." The bartender was still wiping the bar, but when he looked up, the fire that smoldered in his eyes kept Charlie from asking for any kind of elaboration.

The bartender wiped his hands on his apron, grabbed two dirty glasses in his bony fists, and moved to the far end of the bar to wash them. When he passed by the mirror, he cast no reflection, but Charlie dismissed it as a trick of the lighting, just as he had dismissed the disappearing shadows in the booths behind him. Perhaps, even, it was the drink in his hand, and the three before it. He hadn't been able to focus on anything all evening. All the shapes in the bar had fuzzy edges, making background and foreground images sift into one another.

Charlie liked that. He hated things that fought for his attention. He hated the screaming neon lights and the blaring colors advertisers used to grab and hold his attention. Even without the drinks that were numbing his stomach, Charlie would have felt comfortable in a bar like this.

And he liked the quiet. He didn't disco, and he disliked the Cowboy music that dominated most non-dancing bars. He had never seen a juke box in the bar, never heard the clink of quarters dropping into a juke box's stomach, and he was perfectly willing to leave it that way.

Charlie had been to the bar every night that week. He knew where it was, and each night he'd searched out the same tattered red bar stool and watched himself in the mirror as he drank.

The mirror was half as long as the bar, boxed in at each end by shelves of bottles. The lamps in the ceiling cast a dull yellow glow over the top few rows of bottles, and kept his reflection from being as clear as it could be.

The third night he came in, the bartender had leaned over the worn wood of the bar after Charlie had spent half an hour lamenting the departure of his wife. "You're my property now, Mr. Walker. Once you've started coming to my bar, you'll never stop," the bartender had said.

"Why not?" Charlie's depression had been near its peak that night, and he had not been prepared for word games with a sloppy bartender.

"I've been here a long time. I know people." The bartender had laughed at him and Charlie had vowed not to return to the bar. Of course, he had. There were no other bars in his neighborhood, unless they were hidden on back streets like this one, and he was unable to slake his thirst at home. He couldn't stand being in the condominium where thoughts of his wife haunted him.

He had never noticed this bar until the night his wife left him. He had come home late that night and found her note. By the time he'd exhausted his supply of scotch, the corner store was closed and he wandered around the streets until he'd found himself in front of the bar.

The bar. It had no name. No neon lights flashing beer brand names at the night. No loud music erupting through the doorway. A naked bulb swaying in the breeze had been all that illuminated the amber glass of the doorway, and the word "bar" that someone had so carefully stenciled on the glass.

When the bartender appeared to refill his glass, Charlie stopped him. "No more," he said. "I used the last of my savings to make the condo payment. I haven't got the money."

The bartender filled the tumbler. "Don't worry, your credit is good here. Drink what you want."

Charlie accepted the drink without comment.

While they were talking, a stranger in a blue suit entered the bar and found a stool at the far end of the bar from Charlie. He was the only other customer Charlie had seen in the bar all week. The bartender moved to serve him.

The stranger was familiar, but Charlie didn't know him.

Charlie knew his type, though. The elbows of the stranger's blue suit were worn to a shine much like his own, and the ill-fitting shoulders testified to the suit's purchase off the rack at Sears or JCPenney's. The tie was thinner than fashion dictated, and the shoes were polished to a glossy black. The hair, cut shorter than most, was greased back in a poor attempt to hide a generous bald spot. The face was old beyond its wearer's years, deep folds worn into the skin from too much worry.

Michael Bracken

Charlie knew his type all right. He was one of them. A corporate executive who never rose beyond a minor position with a long title. Too many years had seen him passed over when promotion time came. He could feel empathy for the stranger, and he watched as the stranger drank. His gaze was never returned.

When the bartender returned to Charlie's end of the bar, Charlie asked, "You don't get many customers, do you?"

"This place is hard to find. Very few people come in here."

"Yeah," Charlie sighed. "I know."

Charlie watched the bartender drift back to the stranger, returning only as often as Charlie's tumbler needed refilling. He could see the stranger talking, the bartender leaning against the bar, listening and idly polishing the worn wood. Charlie couldn't hear them, but he wondered how many times that scene had been repeated. How many hands had picked up how many tumblers from the bar? How many times had the bartender stood polishing the bar in his distracted manner while some customer sat slowly intoxicating himself and spinning tales of woe?

Hours passed that way and finally the stranger stood up to leave. Charlie reached out as the stranger passed him. He wanted to say something to the stranger, wanted to tell him to find another place to drink, but he couldn't get the words out. The stranger passed through the door without ever noticing Charlie and was soon lost to the night.

Charlie swallowed the last of his drink. He was through for the evening. He stood to leave.

"I wouldn't bother." The bartender was watching him.

Charlie moved to the door and put his fist around the handle. Then he twisted the knob.

Canvas Bleeding

The door was locked.

He turned to look at the bartender. He wanted to go home. He wanted the door unlocked so he could leave.

The bartender was leaning against the inside of the bar, his thin lips locked in a tight smile. "Have you ever read the fine print on those contests? The ones where you send in a slogan or a limerick for a new product?"

Charlie shook his head.

"They all say the same thing," the bartender continued.

"And what's that?"

The bartender pointed.

Charlie stood and looked at the amber glass of the door. Under the word "bar," painted on the glass to be read from the other side of the door, was another sentence. He read it twice and wondered why he'd never noticed it before. "All entries become property of the judges."

"You can't leave now," the bartender said.

"But..." Charlie started. He looked at the door and twisted the knob again.

"I've a new entry to judge, Mr. Walker. Would you care for a booth?"

Heirloom

*T*ommy ran around the corner of the house clutching the glowing gem in one hand and a plastic rifle in the other.

"Bang, bang: you're dead," Tommy shouted as he raised the rifle at Wayne and squeezed the trigger. Wayne sank to the lawn and lay in a heap as Tommy ran past. Even though he should have been making the customary ten count, Tommy heard nothing from Wayne but a soft gurgling.

He stopped at the back gate and breathed hard. With one eye on Wayne to be sure he wasn't ambushed by a suddenly undead enemy, Tommy eased open the gate and took a quick look down the alley. Seeing only the next-door-neighbor lady pulling weeds out of her lawn, he darted across the alley, ran behind the neighbor's boat and crawled underneath it. From there he had a nearly unobstructed view down the alley to the corner and, with the woodpile to one side and the garage wall to the other, he was nearly hidden from view.

He wiped the sweat from his brow with the back of

his left hand and then opened his fist to look at the blood-red gem. It glowed in its silver setting. Just then, out of the corner of his eye, he saw Joey walking cautiously up the alley, a small cloud of dust following his feet as they scuffed in the gravel. Tommy closed his fist and drew the plastic rifle to his shoulder. He took careful aim. "Bang," he shouted, knowing his shot had been true to the heart. "You're dead."

Joey stumbled back and fell into the neighbor lady's sawdust pile. His glasses were twisted on his face and the cap gun he had been carrying lay inches from his outstretched fingers. He lay silent as Tommy crawled out from under the boat and ran to the deserted house on the corner.

Tommy didn't bother to wonder why his friend hadn't started counting out loud the moment he was hit. Tommy wasn't going to wait around and have Joey try a surprise attack the instant he'd finished the mandatory ten count.

With a typical disregard for his mother's orders to stay away from the decaying house, Tommy stumbled over the piles of broken bricks and dropped through the open cellar door to the dusty cement floor.

"Who's that?" said a voice from behind the broken barrel of a plastic submachine gun.

"It's me," Tommy replied, standing still until the sandy-haired boy behind the submachine gun could step out of the shadows and look at him. "Who'd you think it was, Charlie?"

"We can't take any chances, you know, or they'll blow us away," said Charlie. He lowered the gun and motioned for Tommy to follow him back into the shadows. "Come on."

Tommy crept after him and sat down in the dust with his back against the cellar wall and the rifle across his lap. "Where's Grant?" he asked.

"In old lady Harris' hedge, last time I saw him."

"Jeez, where'd you get that?" Charlie asked as Tommy set the glowing gem on the floor between them.

"It was up in the attic with a whole bunch of other stuff. You should see what's up in our attic," Tommy said. The gem and its silver setting had once been part of his grandmother's necklace, but the thin silver chain which had anchored it to her neck had long been lost.

"Can I *touch* it?" Charlie reached out with one grimy hand.

"Sure."

Charlie's fingers slowly encircled the gem and he lifted it carefully. "How come it glows like that?" he asked. He turned the gem over and over in his hands.

"I dunno." Tommy shifted his position against the wall and scratched at the scar on his shoulder.

"Can I have it?" Charlie asked anxiously.

"No." Tommy snatched it from Charlie's hands and stuffed it in his pocket.

"Please?" Charlie whined. "I'll give you my moth collection and both of my big toads and my model of the lunar module."

"No," Tommy said smugly. "It's mine."

Just then they heard a noise outside and both of them immediately returned their attention to the game they were playing. Tommy whispered, "Go over there and cover me. I'm going out."

Charlie crabwalked across the basement floor, kneeled behind a busted packing crate, and motioned to Tommy that he was in position. When Tommy saw Charlie wave his arm, he jumped up and dashed across the basement to the cellar door. Carefully he eased his tangle of brown hair over the edge of the concrete cellar wall and found himself staring into Susan's freckled face.

"Can I play Army, too?" she asked. Her mouth was

Michael Bracken

stuck in its perpetual pout.

"No," Tommy told her. "Go home and play with your dolls." He turned and yelled back down the cellar at Charlie. "Come on, let's get out of here. Susan found us and she'll probably tell Joey where we are."

Forgetting about Charlie, Tommy leaped from the cellar, ran around the house and down the stairway in front. A woman screamed, but Tommy was so intent on getting away from Susan that he didn't hear it.

Tommy had taken things from his grandmother's trunk before, but nothing had ever fascinated him as much as the blood-red gem in its silver setting. Holding it made him feel good. It made him feel whole, like a part of him was missing when the gem wasn't close.

He was stretched out on a tree limb looking at the gem when he heard the siren. When the blue and white police car slowed down and turned into the alley, Tommy climbed down from the tree to see what all the excitement was about. Figuring an event like this called for a temporary truce, he let the plastic rifle drag in the dirt behind him.

At the end of the alley he saw the next-door-neighbor lady shaking her head as a fat policeman spoke to her. As he drew closer, Tommy could see another policeman bending over Joey's still body. Around them stood a few of the neighbors.

"What's going on?" Tommy asked as he sat beside Charlie in the shade of the neighbor's boat. He scratched at his shoulder again. It had been bothering him all afternoon.

"I dunno." Charlie pulled a soggy piece of bubblegum from his pocket. "Want half?"

"Sure." Tommy let the plastic rifle fall to the ground.

"I don't know what happened," they could hear the neighbor lady say to the policeman. "I was working in my garden. When I came out here to get some sawdust

Canvas Bleeding

I saw him just laying there. God, he looks awful. Can I go now, please?"

"Go on," said the fat policeman. "I don't think we'll need to ask you any more questions."

The neighbor lady looked ill as she turned and rushed into the house.

"I'm going to look around," said the fat policeman to his partner.

Tommy pulled the glowing gem from his pocket and rubbed it between his hands. "You wanna *touch* it?" he taunted Charlie.

When Charlie moved his hands toward the gem, Tommy pulled it away, jumped up and ran down the alley. Charlie followed him.

They were too far away to hear when the fat policeman called out to his partner. "Hey, I just found another kid."

*T*ommy lay hidden by old lady Harris' hedge, the barrel of his rifle just barely sticking out from the greenery. He could see down the hill to the sidewalk, but it had been quite a while since he'd seen any of the other guys.

He scratched at the scar on his shoulder. It had been itching since he'd first started playing Army that afternoon.

Tommy had worn that scar ever since his grandmother died. She'd torn the necklace from her throat, snapping the delicate silver chain, and had offered it to him. "It's yours," she'd said. "It always goes to the youngest."

When he got close enough to reach out for the gem, she grabbed him by the arm and scratched his shoulder

71

with it. The cut was barely half an inch long, but it was deep enough to draw a few drops of blood to the surface. She said something in Arabic, the language she'd grown up with in Alexandria, but Tommy didn't understand.

He looked at the cut on his shoulder. "Why'd you do that, Grandma?"

"You must be one with the stone," she said. She sucked in a ragged breath and pointed at a small scar on her left wrist. "My great grandfather gave it to me many years ago."

His own scar was nearly invisible now, and Tommy had never told his mother about that day. His grandmother had died a few hours later, and Tommy's mother had packed all of her things away.

Susan turned the corner and came walking up the street. Tommy drew a bead on her with his rifle, and he followed her movements up the street toward him. But he didn't fire. She wasn't playing Army with them, and he knew better than to shoot a civilian.

"I could've killed you," Tommy said as she drew abreast of his hiding place.

"I'm not playing Army with you."

"That's why I didn't shoot," Tommy said. "Where'd everybody go?"

"I don't know. I haven't seen Joey since lunch."

*T*ommy crawled out from under the hedge. It didn't seem like there was anybody left to play Army with.

His clothes were filthy when his mother called him in for dinner, and he was told to leave his dirty clothes on the back porch. Tommy was wearing only his undershorts when he walked through the kitchen on the way to the bathroom, and his mother noticed the gem in his hand.

"Where'd you get that?" she demanded. She grabbed his hand and forced open his fingers.

"I dunno," Tommy said. He stared down at his feet.

"Did you go up in the attic?" Her eyes were cold and hard as they asked the question.

"No," he said softly.

"Tell me the truth," she demanded. She shook him by the shoulders. "Did you get this out of the attic?"

Tears were streaming down his cheeks and dripping silently to the floor as he stuttered, "Y . . . yes."

"Out of Grandma's trunk?"

"Yes." She was hurting his shoulders.

"Get to your room," she shouted, releasing him. "Now!"

*T*ommy always played in the attic when no one was home, just as he'd gone to the abandoned house down the street when he'd wanted to hide while playing Army. He had been spending time in the attic ever since he grew tall enough to reach the lock on the attic door. But his mother had never yelled at him, nor shaken him so hard before. Tommy waited in his room, wiping the tears away from his cheeks, angry at his mother for the pain in his shoulders.

He heard his mother's footsteps as she came back down from the attic, and he knew she'd returned the necklace to Grandma's trunk. She always returned Grandma's things to the attic after he got them out. And more than anything else, Tommy liked playing with his grandmother's things.

Tommy never had much of a chance to get to know

Michael Bracken

his grandmother. She died when he was only four, but he knew from pictures of her and from the few memories he had of her, that the gem had been the only piece of jewelry she ever wore. Tommy's mother said it had been in the family for generations. It was an heirloom, and, after it was too late, she said it should have been buried with his grandmother. Tommy's mother said it didn't belong in the family anymore. Society had outgrown all of grandmother's Old World superstitions. They had become only so much hocus-pocus and, despite grandmother's stories of the past, Tommy's mother had never believed in supernatural powers. But she didn't want the gem and had packed it away with the rest of his grandmother's things.

And she did her best to keep Tommy away from *all* of grandmother's things. He was too young to know the difference between reality and an old woman's mutterings on her death bed.

A child's imagination is a powerful force.

Tommy pulled on a pair of cutoffs. When he heard his mother rinsing a pan in the kitchen, Tommy slipped out of his room and, with all the stealth he had learned playing Army, he snuck up the attic steps.

His mother had locked the trunk, but the lock was old and rusted. Tommy was determined to retrieve the necklace. It was his. Grandmother had given it to him.

He pried at the lock with a piece of pipe. When the lock finally gave way with a pop, Tommy held his breath for a long moment, hoping his mother was too busy to hear the sound of the rusty lock breaking.

He reached into the trunk and his hand found the gem immediately. He clasped it tight and headed back down the stairs.

His mother was waiting at the foot of the staircase. "I've been calling you for two minutes," she said. "What have you been doing up there." It wasn't a question. It was a demand.

Tommy opened his hand. "I got Grandma's necklace."

It was a defiant gesture and she slapped him for it. Blood trickled inside his mouth.

"Damn it, Tommy. I've told you to stay away from there and I mean it." She reached for the gem in Tommy's hand. She was going to take it away from him again. He could see that.

His shoulders hurt, the blood in his mouth tasted warm, and he hated his mother then, for just that instant. "I wish you were —"

"Tommy, no!" she screamed, finally believing.

"— dead."

The Man at the Window

"He's there again."

"Where?"

"At the window. Watching us."

Maureen turned toward the window. She saw only the green expanse of the back yard. "There's no one there."

"He's gone now."

Maureen looked across the kitchen table at her daughter. The blonde second-grader was toying with her peas, picking at them with her fingers.

"Finish your dinner, Angel," Maureen said quietly.

The tiny kitchen was silent except for the sound of Maureen's silverware scraping against her plate.

"Mommy?"

"Yes, dear?" Maureen swallowed a sliver of pork chop. The mushroom sauce had almost burned while she prepared dinner; the chop was tough and over-

Michael Bracken

cooked.

"Why does he watch me?"

Maureen shrugged. She'd been through all this before. The psychiatrist had said her daughter would grow out of it.

"I saw him at school yesterday."

"What was he doing?"

"Watching me."

"Where was he?" Maureen laid her fork aside and reached for her coffee mug. She turned the chipped side away from her chapped lips and took a sip.

"On the other side of the fence. By the woods."

"Did you tell the teacher about him?" Maureen asked.

"Yes."

"What did she do?"

"She didn't see him. He was gone before she looked."

Maureen nodded and a lock of hair — hazel and flecked with grey — fell across her forehead. Her daughter's teachers had been told about the man and about the psychiatrist's report. They had been very good about it all.

"Have the other children ever seen him?"

"No," Angel said. "He isn't interested in the other kids."

Maureen nodded again, took a second sip from her coffee mug, and set it down. The first time Angel had mentioned the man, Maureen had warned her about taking candy from strangers. The second time Angel mentioned the man, Maureen had called the police. There was nothing the police could do: nothing had happened. They warned Maureen about flashers and perverts and told her to keep a close watch on Angel. Maureen had been frightened then, had been extra cautious everywhere she took her daughter. When Angel began seeing the man at school, the teachers had recommended a psychiatrist. No one had seen the man but Angel.

"When I walked home from school today, he followed me."

Maureen glanced up at her daughter. The man had never followed Angel before. "All the way home?"

"Three blocks," Angel said. "The last three blocks."

"Did he touch you?"

Angel shook her head. "He never touches me."

The kitchen was silent again. Angel poked at her pork chop. Maureen stared at the delicate blue pattern on the edge of her plate. In the morning she planned to phone Dr. Bates and make another appointment for her daughter. He'd promised that the man would soon go away, but he hadn't.

"Are you finished eating?" Maureen finally asked. Her daughter had taken only a few bites of the meal.

Angel nodded. "I'm not hungry."

"You can go wash up now."

Angel slid from the wooden chair and padded barefoot across the linoleum floor. She stopped at the edge of the living room carpet. "Mommy?"

"Yes?" Maureen turned to look at her daughter.

"I love you."

"I love you, too."

Angel disappeared into the living room. A moment later Maureen heard the water running in the bathroom sink.

Maureen quickly cleared the table, stacking the dirty dinner dishes beside the stainless steel sink. Then she followed her daughter's path out of the kitchen, across the living room, and into the bathroom. Angel was drying her hands on the fluffy beige towel.

"He talked to me when we got home," Angel said.

"What did he say?" Maureen was worried. Angel had first seen the man a few weeks after her father's death, and had seen him only a half-dozen times when Maureen had taken her to see the psychiatrist. Dr. Bates had explained the man away with his psychiatric mumbo-jumbo and Maureen had believed him. It was easier than believing the man existed.

"He said he wanted to take me to see Daddy."

Maureen helped her daughter out of her yellow and white school dress and into a faded pink nightgown.

"Would you like to see Dr. Bates tomorrow?"

Angel cocked her head to one side. Blonde hair fell like a plumb-line to her shoulder. "Why?"

"He likes to talk to you about the man."

"He doesn't believe me," the little girl answered. "I can tell."

"Will you talk to him if I make an appointment?"

Angel shrugged.

Maureen scooped up her daughter and carried her into the living room where they both plopped onto the overstuffed couch. "Do you want me to read you a book?"

The little girl nodded. They snuggled together on the couch just like they'd done every night since Bill's death. Maureen read a handful of books, about Care Bears and Smurfs and Bugs Bunny. Then she carried her half-asleep daughter into the little girl's bedroom and laid her slender body down on the bed. She pulled the covers up and carefully tucked them around her.

"Goodnight, sweetheart," Maureen said.

"Good-bye, Mommy," Angel said sleepily.

Maureen looked down at Angel, half-hidden in the dark shadows of the room. "Goodnight," she whispered, correcting her daughter.

Maureen pulled Angel's bedroom door nearly closed, then made her way down the hall to her own bedroom. It was early, but she'd had a hard day coping with the demands of the job she'd been forced to find

Canvas Bleeding

after her husband's death. It felt good when she stripped off her clothes and slipped between the cool sheets. Before she snapped off the lamp next to her bed, Maureen left a note to phone Dr. Bates.

The next morning, the hum of her alarm roused Maureen from a deep and undisturbed sleep. When she reached to switch the alarm off, she saw the note pad and the message she'd left for herself.

She slipped on a robe and made her way down the hall to her daughter's bedroom. She pushed the heavy wooden door open, expecting to see Angel's face buried in the white pillow. Instead, she found the bed empty.

Maureen called out her daughter's name, pushed the door all the way open, and saw the curtains moving gently with the morning breeze. The window had been opened from the inside. She stumbled across an abandon teddy bear as she ran to the window and forced the curtains aside. She stared out across the back lawn.

Then Maureen screamed Angel's name across the neighborhood.

Again.

And again.

And again.

Father's Day

A tidal wave of heat swept across the small Illinois town of Kolb. The regulars — old men with nothing else to do but putter in their gardens — sat at the counter in the town drugstore comparing the heat wave to the summer of '17 and the summer of '55. At the town's only service station, a teenage attendant dropped 50 cents into the soda machine and swore when he realized the refrigeration unit had broken and his soda was as hot as he. At a small farm on the edge of town, a stooped old woman collected eggs, carefully placed them in baskets, and placed the baskets in a child's red wagon. She wiped sweat from her forehead with the back of her hand.

On Hill Street seven-year-old Jamie Stiles struggled with a heavy cardboard box, finally freeing it from the tightly-packed trunk of his stepfather's Pontiac. His arms barely reached around the box and he leaned back to counterbalance its weight as he climbed the concrete steps up to his new home. As he reached the top, sweat ran from his forehead, stinging his pale blue eyes. He stumbled, dropped the box, and watched it bounce down fourteen steps to the sidewalk, his mother's collection of drinking glasses shattering in tiny explosions each time the box struck a step.

"Damn it, Jamie." His mother burst from the ramshackle bungalow, her thin face crimson with anger. She clamped a rough hand around Jamie's arm and hauled him to his feet. Her other hand lashed across his cheek. "Your feet too big?"

Jamie stared up at his mother. Her brown hair hung limply to her shoulders; sweat beaded on her forehead.

She struck him again. "I told you to be careful, didn't I?"

"Yes," Jamie said hoarsely.

"I'll teach you to be careful." She raised her hand a third time and Jamie prepared himself for the blow.

The screen door slammed. Jamie's stepfather stood on the porch watching them.

"You mind your own business, Frank," she said.

"He's your kid, Sara." Frank stepped back inside the house.

She turned to Jamie. "You clean that mess up. Then you bring in the other boxes."

Jamie twisted from his mother's grip and hurried down the steps, his over-sized Goodwill sneakers slapping against the hot concrete. Broken glass had spilled out through the burst corner of the box and Jamie stooped to pick it up.

A broom and a metal dustpan clattered to the sidewalk beside him. Jamie looked up the hill and saw his mother silhouetted against the mid-afternoon sun, the rolled-up sleeves of his stepfather's workshirt adding unnatural bulk to her upper arms.

"Use your brains," she said. Then she turned and retreated into the house, yelling, "When the hell you gonna have that air-conditioner working, Frank?"

Canvas Bleeding

Alone at the bottom of the steps, Jamie used a dirty hand to wipe a tear from the corner of his eye, feeling the stinging pain as his fingertips slid across his swollen cheek. He wiped his wet hand on the front of his sleeveless grey sweatshirt, then looked down at the tracks of blood on his knee where he'd scraped it on the step.

For a moment he watched the blood coagulate.

On the corner, half a block away, a stooped old woman with a red wagon watched Jamie.

*L*ater, sitting on his unmade bed in the sweltering house, staring at the blank blue walls of his new room, Jamie picked at the scab on his knee and remembered the questions his father used to ask when they returned home from the duck pond on Sunday afternoons.

"How'd Jamie get this bruise?"

"He fell," his mother said without looking.

"He falls a lot, doesn't he?"

"He's a clumsy kid. I've told you that before."

"He's not clumsy when he's with me."

"You're so damned over-protective; how could he ever get hurt with you?"

"Maybe he needs protection, Sara."

"From what?"

"From you."

"Bullshit."

Jamie's father shook his head and scooped Jamie into his arms. As they headed toward Jamie's bedroom, his father said, "I'll protect you, champ. Just call me when you need me."

Michael Bracken

Jamie's new home had stood empty for months, barely cared for by owners who had given up all hope of renting it. One afternoon Frank arrived, told them how he'd just been hired as the mechanic at the town's only service station, and offered them a cash deposit. The owners didn't hesitate to take Frank's money.

The day after Jamie's family moved into the two-bedroom crackerbox at the top of the hill, his mother answered a heavy knock at the front door. A stooped old woman in a housedress stood on the porch. She smelled heavily of garlic. Her long, grey hair floated in wisps about her face as the afternoon breeze caught it.

The old woman held a small basket of eggs at arm's length, offering them to Jamie's mother. "Fresh eggs." Her voice quavered a bit. "Fifty cents a dozen." She cocked her head to one side, as if it were too heavy to hold upright, and waited for a response.

Jamie touched the back of his mother's thigh. She glanced down and saw him staring at the Egg Lady.

"How about it Jamie?" she asked. "Do you think your father would like fresh eggs?"

Quietly, Jamie whispered, "He's not my father."

Jamie's mother turned to him. "Don't say that Jamie. Frank *is* your father now."

Jamie shook his head without glancing away from the Egg Lady. "No he isn't. My father's gone."

"We'll talk about it later, Jamie. This isn't the time."

"I deliver Tuesday and Friday," the Egg Lady said. "Fresh eggs." She watched the boy.

"Get my purse, Jamie."

He backed away from the door, then turned and ran to the kitchen. He returned with his mother's dog-eared leather purse. She reached in, retrieved a pair of quarters, and handed them to the old woman.

Canvas Bleeding

"Tuesday and Friday," the Egg Lady repeated. "You leave the money and the basket on the porch; I leave a new basket of eggs. No money; no eggs."

Jamie's mother nodded and took the basket from the woman's outstretched hand, her fingers just barely grazing the old woman's knotted knuckles. She jerked back, shivering.

"You embarrassed me," Jamie's mother told him as she closed the door.

Jamie climbed on the couch and stared out the window without responding. He watched as the Egg Lady slowly made her way down the concrete steps to the sidewalk. She bent to retrieve the handle of a child's red wagon, then pulled it up the street out of sight.

"We've had this talk before, damn it," his mother continued. "Frank is your father now. There's nothing you can do to change that."

The Egg Lady disappeared around the corner and Jamie turned to face his mother. He could still smell garlic.

His mother lashed out with her hand. Jamie ducked to the side and her hand passed over his head into a lamp on the end table, knocking it to the floor.

"Now look what you made me do!"

As he jumped to the floor, she grabbed the back of his collar.

*J*amie sat sullenly at the dinner table that night while his mother told Frank about the Egg Lady.

"You bought eggs from her?" Frank slammed his fork against his plate. Mashed potatoes splattered across the end of the table.

"I thought you'd like fresh eggs," Jamie's mother

said. Her fork hovered midway between her plate and her mouth.

Jamie silently watched them. He didn't eat.

"You didn't ask me, did you?"

"No."

"This time," Frank said. "This time I'll let it go." He paused and breathed heavily for a moment. "Next time you ask. Understand?"

"Like hell I will. I don't need your permission for anything."

Frank stared at her without speaking.

"It wasn't supposed to be like this, Frank."

"Like what?"

"Arguing. You promised."

Frank snorted. "You married me 'cause I'm a good fuck. That's all I promised."

"And you haven't been too good at that lately."

"You ain't been no sex queen yourself."

Jamie's mother looked down at her plate and didn't look up again until Jamie asked to be excused.

He hurried to his room, reached under his mattress, and found the photo his mother had taken on his second birthday. In it, Jamie, face smeared with chocolate cake, kissed his father.

The photo, crumpled once but smoothed flat by Jamie, was all he had left. After his father's death, Jamie's mother destroyed the family photo albums, ripped them apart and crumpled all the photos of his father. The photo in his hand was all Jamie'd managed to save from the trash.

He stared at the photo and remembered the last time he had been alone with his father. He remembered the cloudless powder-blue wash of sky above the cemetery. His father held his hand and led him across the manicured lawn to the pond. Ducks gathered around them, quacking and honking at the loaves of stale bread his father carried.

They sat cross-legged on the cool grass. Imitating his father's posture, Jamie tried to force his stomach out so it would roll over his belt. He couldn't do it.

After opening the first loaf of bread, his father handed Jamie a stale crust. Jamie laughed, tore the bread in half, and threw both halves to the ducks. Jamie laughed again as his father ran a firm hand through his hair, wrapped one meaty arm around his shoulder, and pulled him close in an affectionate bear hug.

When the bread was gone, Jamie's father gathered the empty wrappers and squeezed them into a loose ball. Then Jamie crawled onto his father's lap, fighting for space with the wide belly already there. Jamie snuggled against his father's chest, listening to the heart thump inside.

"I'll always be there when you need me, champ," his father said.

His father had always been there for Jamie, coming home from work with his tie hanging askew, ready to pull Jamie off his feet and swing him in the air; waking early Saturday mornings to watch cartoons and ready in the afternoon to push the park swings for Jamie and his friends; buying loaves of stale bread on Sunday mornings to feed the ducks at the cemetery.

When they returned home that day, Jamie's mother hadn't yet returned from church. While they sat at the table eating sandwiches, his mother returned. She smelled of sex and cigarettes.

"You've been with him again, haven't you?"

She turned her back on his father.

"Why?"

"You wouldn't understand."

"Try me," he said. "Just once, try to explain to me the things that go on inside your head."

And Jamie remembered his last visit to the cemetery

Michael Bracken

when the men lowered his father's casket into the ground, the plot so close to the pond that ducks stood at his feet during the service.

Then later his mother refused to take him to the cemetery, acting like his father had never existed.

Jamie hid the photo under his mattress.

A few weeks later Jamie sat on the bottom step and waited. He held an empty egg basket and two quarters. It was Jamie's job to wait for the Egg Lady's arrival, to count the eggs, and to pay her. It was a job Jamie enjoyed because the Egg Lady always stopped to talk to him.

When she finally arrived, her red wagon creaking behind her, Jamie held up his empty basket and the two quarters. She dropped the quarters into her pocket, replaced the empty basket with a full one, then reached deep into another pocket and pulled out a small silver object.

She offered it to Jamie.

"What is it?"

"Take it. Put it on the ground."

Tentatively, Jamie took the shiny silver toy — an over-sized jack polished bright to sparkle in the sunlight, as light and fragile as aluminum foil.

"Put it down," she told him again.

Carefully, Jamie placed the jack on the concrete step. It spun, the sun sparkling off the silver arms. He grabbed the jack and it stopped. He placed it on the step and it spun. He picked it up again and it stopped.

Jamie looked at the Egg Lady.

"It's yours," she said.

He set the jack back on the step and watched it spin.

"What happened to your father?" she asked.

Canvas Bleeding

He told her about the cemetery and the duck pond.

The Egg Lady smiled and pulled the wagon up the street to her next delivery.

*I*n the living room the next afternoon, Jamie's mother saw him playing with the spinning silver jack. She grabbed the toy with one hand, Jamie's wrist with the other.

"Where'd you get this?" she demanded.

"The Egg Lady gave it to me."

She crushed the toy in her hand. "Don't lie to me."

"But —"

"You stole it."

She dropped the toy, reached into her pocket, then held Jamie's palm over the flame of her disposable lighter. Jamie bit his bottom lip as the flesh of his hand slowly blistered.

"Don't lie to me."

Jamie shook his head.

"Where did you get it?"

"I . . . I stole it," he whispered.

When she released Jamie's wrist, he pulled his hand from the flame. Tears formed at the corners of his eyes, as Jamie ran to his room to nurse his hand in silence, the crumpled photo of his father his only companion.

*T*uesday morning Jamie sat on the bottom step and watched the Egg Lady approach. On the back of her wagon sat a brown duck with a thin leather leash around its neck.

"This is for you," she said. She held the leash out for

Michael Bracken

Jamie to take.

He stared at her blankly. He was wary; his hand still throbbed with pain. Cocking his head to one side, Jamie looked at the duck. He'd never had a pet before.

Finally, Jamie took the end of the leash from the Egg Lady's gnarled hand.

"If you had a wish," she said, "what would it be?"

"Like fairy tales?" Jamie asked. He'd heard of fairy tales; stories about gingerbread men, red riding hoods, rumpled stilt skins. He thought. "I'd want a friend."

"I'm your friend."

Jamie nodded.

He tugged at the duck's leash. It hopped up the steps and stood beside him. He wrapped one thin arm around the bird.

"Does she have a name?"

"He," corrected the Egg Lady. "No he doesn't." Wisps of white hair fell across her craggy face. She brushed them away.

"Can I give him one?"

"If you want."

Jamie rubbed the back of the duck with his good hand, feeling the feathers between his fingers.

"How about Champ?"

"That's a good name."

He rubbed the duck again. "I wish my hand didn't hurt."

The Egg Lady examined Jamie's palm when he held it out.

"I have something," she said. She reached deep into one pocket of her housedress and removed a bottle of ointment. She carefully rubbed some onto Jamie's palm. "Give it time."

Jamie sniffed his hand. It smelled of garlic, like the Egg Lady.

"Anything else?" she asked.

Jamie thought hard, then shook his head.

"You take your time," she said. The Egg Lady straightened. From her red wagon, she took a basket filled with two dozen eggs.

Jamie accepted the basket, gave the Egg Lady the crumpled dollar from his pocket, and handed her the empty basket. Then he slowly climbed the steps to the house. The duck followed at the end of its leash.

A half hour later Jamie's mother returned from the store. She saw Jamie holding the duck. "Where the hell'd you get that?"

"From the Egg Lady," Jamie said softly.

"Then it'll make good roasting," his mother said. She grabbed the duck by the neck and pulled it from Jamie's protective grasp. With one swift yank she broke its neck. It flopped in her hands, then she carried the dead bird into the house.

Jamie sat on the front porch, the broken leather leash still dangling from his hand.

At the dinner table that night, his father's photo carefully tucked in his pocket, Jamie picked at his corn and stared at the piece of duck on his plate.

"Crazy old broad came into the station this morning," his stepfather said. "Said she had to go on an important trip. Made me put two new tires on an old pickup that looked like it couldn't cross town without a tow truck."

Jamie considered the piece of duck for a moment, then carefully cleaned all the meat from the wishbone.

"I asked her where she was going in such a rush. She said she was going to the cemetery to visit a friend's father. I told her if the old guy was already dead, she

Michael Bracken

sure didn't need to hurry. He'd still be there when she arrived." Frank laughed at his own joke. Jamie's mother joined him.

Jamie held up the wishbone, one prong in his fist. "Make a wish, Mom."

His mother hesitated, then took the other end in her hand and pulled. The wishbone snapped and the house suddenly grew cold. Jamie's mother shivered and he smiled for the first time in four years.

His father was coming to protect him.

All the World's a Rage

"My wife wanted a new doormat, so I got cloned."

Eddie Sims switched off the portable black-and-white TV. Two weeks earlier that sentence had taken Eddie an hour to peck out on his portable typewriter. A week earlier it had added five dollars to his bank account. Now it was playing coast-to-coast on "The Tonight Show," and it was Maxwell taking the bows and receiving the applause.

Eddie had never met Maxwell, though he'd watched over the years as Maxwell's appearances on talk shows, game shows, and variety shows had gradually increased. Eddie listened to the laughter Maxwell received, laughter that welled up from inside people instead of from the guts of unfeeling machines.

Michael Bracken

His words. Maxwell's voice. They had been a team for seven years.

After slowly sucking up the last dregs of cold coffee from the chipped mug Mrs. Dunfee had left on the table for him, Eddie struggled to roll a white index card into his typewriter. Maxwell needed more jokes.

The sun had fought its way over the horizon before Eddie had six jokes that satisfied him. They had been carefully typed, one joke to a card, and he inserted the cards into a small white envelope addressed to Maxwell's New York condo. With twisted fingers, Eddie lay the envelope on the corner of the yellow and chrome kitchen table for Mrs. Dunfee to take to the Post Office on her daily walk.

Tired and uncomfortable in his seat, Eddie let his chin drop to his chest. His neck hurt from the strained effort of keeping his head upright as he typed. Slowly, his breathing a fight against the leather straps binding him to the wheelchair, Eddie found sleep.

A week later Maxwell sat next to Jay Leno. His bulbous, pock-marked nose was a ski slope for the sweat that ran down his forehead and dripped onto his red plaid jacket.

". . . don't have any luck at all," he was saying. "I went into a restaurant last week and ordered a tossed green salad. The waiter fixed a green salad, then he tossed it at me." Maxwell paused while the live audience roared its approval. "So I asked for the Chef's Surprise. He came out of the kitchen and showed me stag films of my wife."

"What about the new punk rock dance?" Leno prompted.

"It's called the Maxwell. You lay on the dance floor and people walk all over you."

During the commercial break, Maxwell left the stage to catch a cab.

The next morning, wearing only a pair of blue boxer shorts, Maxwell dropped his bulk into a chrome and plastic kitchen chair and sorted through the mail until he came to the envelope with the Blackwood postmark. Without reading them, Maxwell counted the number of index cards in the envelope and quickly wrote out a personal check for thirty dollars. He folded the check in half and stuffed it into Eddie's return envelope.

An ugly squab of a man, Maxwell belched into the back of his hand and felt his stomach do calisthenics. He'd veered from his special diet the previous night and his body rebelled against him. Even doctor's orders couldn't keep him from nibbling at the rich food served at the parties he'd been attending the past few years. His back pockets, never close together, had been spreading further apart.

He rose from the chair in search of antacids when the white wall phone jangled. He answered with a simple hello.

"Maxie? It's Jack. I've got you booked on a talk show tomorrow night. Have you got any new material?"

Maxwell glanced over at the table. "A few jokes. Not much," he told his agent. He hadn't written any of his own material since Eddie's first envelope had arrived in the mail seven years earlier, and he depended on Eddie's ability to produce new jokes.

"Wife jokes, Maxie," his agent said. "You got any wife jokes?"

Maxwell waddled to the table, the handset carefully tucked between his shoulder and his double chin. He quickly scanned the cards. "A few."

"Good. That's what they want. More wife jokes."

Michael Bracken

While Maxwell was talking, Joan entered the kitchen clad only in a pair of skimpy pink panties. After Maxwell hung up, she asked, "Who was that?"

"Jack," Maxwell told her as he gathered her slender body in his arms, her heavy breasts pressing against his chest. "He's got a talk show for me tomorrow night."

Joan reached up, clasped her arms around the back of his neck, then kissed him firmly. She had been living with Maxwell for the past year, providing him with the companionship he had lacked ever since his ex-wife walked out on him more than nine years previous.

"I rolled over and you weren't there," she whispered hoarsely in his ear. "I almost had to take care of myself."

*T*he bartender convulsed with laughter, his massive, leather-tough hands wrapped around a stained-white apron. "He doesn't have to say a thing," the bartender said as Maxwell performed a monologue on a new variety show. "The way he rolls those pop-eyes just kills me."

Eddie didn't laugh. He couldn't.

"I wonder how he comes up with all that crazy stuff." The bartender let out a whooping laugh at one of Eddie's jokes when Maxwell finished the punch line.

Eddie stared into his beer. It was too much effort to twist his head upward to stare at the tiny television on the wall behind the bar. He knew the words. He could hear the laughter.

"Do you want another one, Eddie? Your tab's still good."

Eddie nodded.

Later, after being wheeled back to his apartment, Eddie spent a long time in front of the typewriter. Each letter was difficult to peck out with his twisted fingers, and the little cards were awkward to insert into the portable's carriage.

By late morning he still hadn't been to sleep, but he had finished another batch of jokes.

"I done the other room," Mrs. Dunfee said from somewhere behind him. She was rail-thin, her blue-grey hair pulled so tightly into a bun that she'd smoothed some of the wrinkles on her forehead. Every morning the widow crossed the street from her house to fix Eddie's breakfast and help him eat it. "You got another one of them letters to mail?"

She reached over his shoulder and snatched the envelope from the corner of the kitchen table. She never read the name or the address, never thought twice about the envelopes she mailed for him, nor about the checks she deposited for him every Friday. Mrs. Dunfee was a simple woman whose life revolved around caring for Eddie and reading the Bible.

"I'll come by later, Eddie," she said, patting him where his shoulder should have been. "You take care now."

*M*axwell was confined to the under-sized dressing room chair. He'd dropped into it after rushing off stage away from the spotlight. He sucked air through puffy blue lips and ran his pudgy fingers through his thinning black hair. The image reflected back at him by the mirror wasn't a pleasant one, and he could see beads of sweat standing at attention on his forehead. He wiped them away with the back of his hand.

The pace had begun to gnaw at him. His heart attack early in the year had been minor and he'd been lucky to keep the news away from the trade journals and

Michael Bracken

gossip columns.

Jack burst through the dressing room door behind Maxwell. He wore a custom-tailored leisure suit and yards of gold chain. "You were terrific, Maxie. Did you hear the applause?"

"I did okay, Jack," he said. "Could you get me some water?"

Maxwell pulled a tablet from the jacket pocket of his plaid suit and placed it on his dry tongue. He washed the pill down with a large swallow of warm water from the glass Jack shoved into his fist.

When Eddie's first envelope of jokes had arrived, Maxwell's career had been taking a dive. He'd just been cut from a local talk show when a football star and one of Charlie's former angels had shown a clip from their latest movie. Maxwell had gotten drunk that afternoon and had stayed drunk all weekend.

The following Monday he'd received Eddie's first envelope. Six jokes were tucked inside, each of them suited perfectly to Maxwell's style. He'd written his first check to Eddie that day, paying his usual fee, just as he'd underpaid all the other writers during his roller-coaster career.

He worked Eddie's material into his act right away, and with a new packet of cards arriving almost every time the mail was delivered, his routine soon consisted entirely of Eddie's work.

A few minutes after swallowing the pill, Maxwell started feeling better and Joan took him back to their hotel room. She laid him back across the hotel bed and slowly pulled his clothes off. Then she bent to kiss him on the forehead, thinking him to be asleep. Surprising her, Maxwell gathered Joan in his arms, pressed his lips against hers, and gave her a firm kiss.

When their lips finally parted, Joan said, "You must be feeling better."

A few days later, Jack argued with Maxwell. "Look," he said, "I've got you booked on a cross-country tour, playing only the biggest venues."

"I just can't do it, Jack," Maxwell said across the expanse of his agent's desk. He sat uncomfortably in one of the guest chairs, his chin sunk into a roll of fat.

"Maxie, even Seinfeld couldn't get a deal like this."

Maxwell sat sullenly for a moment. "Last week I think I had another heart attack —"

"You *what?*" Jack straightened up, his gold chains bouncing off the desk top.

"I didn't tell anybody."

"Shit, Maxie, don't check out now." Maxwell was Jack's only truly successful client, a relationship that was on the verge of making him a millionaire.

A few days later, Maxwell conceded to his agent's demands. "On one condition."

"What?" Jack was weary. He'd been on the phone all morning negotiating Maxwell's part in the new Mel Brooks film.

"Everyday someone picks up the mail at my condo and brings it to me."

"You're crazy, Maxie. It's just bills and junk mail and fan letters from kooks in Duluth. Joan can handle it."

"No, Jack. It has to be brought to me or we don't have a deal."

Jack sat passively behind his desk, not comprehending Maxwell's fixation on the mail. He'd never known about Eddie.

"It's delivered just after nine a.m. Catch the next flight out of La Guardia and you should have it to me that night before the show."

"That's insane." Jack was shaking his head, slowly, careful not to mess up his hair. "Do you realize how much that'll cost?"

Michael Bracken

"Do you?"

"*It*'s closing time, Eddie," the bartender said in his gravel voice. "Do you want somebody to help you home?" Before Eddie could nod, the bartender called out. "Hey, Elbert, you live up that way, don't ya? Eddie needs some help home."

From a booth in the dark recesses of the bar came the response. "Sure thing. I'll be up there in a minute."

"Finish your beer, Eddie," the bartender said, leaning across the bar to adjust Eddie's straw. "We'll get you home just fine."

Blackwood was a small town, barely a blister on the skin of the earth. Hidden from the rest of the world by corn fields and gently rolling hills, it was a town where Eddie could live in peace.

They were all Eddie's friends there. Some, like the bartender, had grown up with Eddie. Others, like Mrs. Dunfee, had helped his mother care for him during his infancy.

When he made his way slowly down the street to the bar every few nights, no one gave him a second glance. And when Mrs. Dunfee took him to the Lutheran church every Sunday morning, even the Reverend shook his hand.

Anywhere else, Eddie wouldn't have survived.

*M*axwell stood center stage, his corpulent body bathed by three spotlights. The audience was on its feet applauding. It wasn't the first standing ovation he'd gotten during the tour, and Maxwell bowed carefully.

Canvas Bleeding

Just that afternoon a network executive had offered Maxwell his own television series and Jack had spent the evening pressuring him to accept.

When he straightened up, Maxwell felt pain shoot down his right arm. He grimaced and bowed again.

"Are you okay, Maxie?" Jack asked backstage. "You look terrible."

"I'll be fine."

Jack led him into the dressing room. "Lay down, Maxie. Take a rest. Maybe I'll cancel tomorrow night's show."

"I'll be okay, Jack. Just give me a minute." Maxwell made his way to the overnight bag on the dressing room table. From an inside pouch he pulled a road map he'd picked up at the airport. He spread the map across the table and studied the tiny print.

"Get me a car," he finally told his agent. "I have to meet someone before it's too late."

Before long the rented Ford was whistling across the Poplar Street Bridge as he left the city behind. Maxwell pushed the seat as far back as he could to accommodate his bulk, and the pedals were just barely within reach of his toes. Still, despite the pain crawling up his arm, he was happy to finally be alone.

The breeze from the open window caught in his thinning hair and plastered it back across his head. Cold air bit at the back of his throat as he inhaled. Tiny snowflakes began dotting the windshield.

He didn't slow the car until an hour had passed and he turned off the interstate to consult his map. Two and a half hours after leaving the stage, Maxwell pulled into Blackwood. The population count on the sign at the edge of town had been smaller than his city block back in New York, and it took only a few minutes to find Eddie's apartment.

The Ford slid to a halt at the curb and Maxwell noted

Michael Bracken

with satisfaction that a light still burned dully in Eddie's apartment. He buttoned his shirt and pulled on his jacket. A half-inch of snow had collected on the streets of Blackwood.

After seven years, Maxwell was determined to meet the writer who had made him a star. He waddled up the walk to the apartment and pounded on the door with his meaty fist.

Across the street, a light snapped on.

Maxwell pounded again.

Eddie looked up from his typing. He didn't often get visitors in the silent hours before dawn. He hadn't paid any attention to the car slowing outside his window, nor to the sound of the car door slamming.

When the pounding came again, Eddie turned his chair toward the door.

"Hey, mister." Mrs. Dunfee, wrapped in a tattered blue robe, stood on her porch with a high-powered flashlight in one gnarled hand, her dead husband's service revolver in the other. She trained the flashlight across the street toward Maxwell. The single shaft of light raped the darkness and pinned his bulky silhouette against Eddie's apartment door. "What're'ya doin' at Eddie's?"

Eddie cautiously opened his front door and found himself facing the back of a red plaid jacket. He could hear Mrs. Dunfee's high, scratchy voice yelling from across the street and he was momentarily caught in the spotlight with the comic.

Maxwell spun around to face Eddie when he heard the door scrape open, stepping forward with his hand outstretched to clasp the hand of the writer who'd rescued his career from the abyss. He caught his breath and his arm jerked backward, his hand involuntarily closing into a fist when he saw Eddie strapped into his wheelchair. From behind, Maxwell appeared as if he was about to strike Eddie. He heard the revolver's roar from across the street and felt a band of pain suddenly tighten across his chest.

"Eddie Sims?" he asked, gasping for breath as he clawed at his chest.

Eddie watched the ugly, overweight, badly dressed comic fall to the porch and scatter the powdery snow. Mrs. Dunfee ran across the street, sliding in her battered house slippers. Her flashlight panned the neighborhood like a spastic strobe as it swung wildly at her side. By the time she reached the porch, Maxwell had expelled his last ragged breath.

Eddie sat silently in his wheelchair watching the comic die. There was nothing Eddie could have done. He had no vocal chords to call for help. His distorted, legless torso had been confined to the wheelchair since childhood, when he'd finally learned to balance himself in a sitting position with the aid of straps around his chest.

Anywhere else he would have been jeered and taunted for his disfigurement, but in Blackwood they protected Eddie from strangers.

*Jerome Edgemont, failing comic, opened the envelope with the offbeat postmark and watched as a half-dozen index cards tumbled to the carpet.

He stooped to pick them up.

Shadow of My Father

My father visits my room each night. He stands naked in the open doorway staring at me, the light from the hallway behind him sending tendrils of his shadow across my bed. I lie facing the wall, my knees drawn up to my chin, pretending to sleep.

Some nights he turns away, returning to the warmth of his own bed, where my mother lies snoring, her greying hair bound up in curlers and her worn flannel gown twisted around the whale-like girth of her body.

Other nights he comes to me, lifting the heavy quilt away from my shoulders and pulling it back. I clutch the thin sheet to my neck, but my father pries it from my grasping fingers. Then he lays behind me on the single bed and kisses the back of my neck. The rough stubble of his beard scratches my shoulder and I wince. That's when he knows I'm awake.

He whispers in the dark, his voice hoarse from

shouting over the pounding rhythm of machinery at the plant, telling me he loves me like he loves Mommy, but he never kisses her, never even touches her. He promises that he'll love me forever if I'm his good little girl and it's a promise that frightens me more now than it did then.

I can't remember him not visiting my room at night. At first he just touched me, touched me in places Mommy said strangers should never be allowed to touch. Then he began kissing me, his thick tongue forcing its way into my mouth and tasting of cigarettes and whiskey.

Later, he made me kiss One-Eyed Jack, and when I gagged on the warm and sticky emissions, my father clamped his work-hardened hand over my mouth to silence me, nearly suffocating me as I struggled to breathe.

As I grew older, he would position himself between my legs and drive One-Eyed Jack deep inside me. I stuffed my fist in my mouth or bit down hard on a pillow to keep from screaming as he tore my insides apart, preventing me from ever becoming a parent. He always drove into me quickly, urgently, finishing moments after he began and leaving me alone in the bed while he padded to the bathroom to cleanse himself.

If my sheets were still damp in the morning, my mother would bend me over her corpulent knee and spank me with a two-inch wide leather belt for wetting the bed, my father watching her but saying nothing about his nocturnal visits.

As my breasts developed, my hips widened, and my pubic hair changed from fluff to coarse black curls, my father's visits to my bed grew increasingly frequent. I once tried to tell my mother about them, but she didn't hear me, perhaps ignoring my reality for one of her own, one in which a middle-aged woman who hadn't completed grade school and who had done little more than keep house and cook meals most of her life had a roof over her head and food in her belly and clothes on her back, a reality in which she sacrificed her only daughter on the altar of self-preservation.

There seemed no escape from my father until one Saturday morning when he was crushed under our aging station wagon. The official report says the car slipped off the jack, but I know better. A simple kick as I passed by, my unconscious doing what my conscious had never been able to do, had sent the jack ratcheting downward. It had taken him hours to die beneath the car, my mother finally discovering his lifeless body early that evening when she returned from an all-day shopping trip to the city with our next-door neighbor.

Yet even now, my father rolls me onto my back and pushes my nightgown up into my armpits, revealing the tiny pink buds of my undeveloped breasts. He strokes my nipples with the callused balls of his thumbs and they stiffen at the attention. I feel his hot breath against my cheek and the thick tube of One-Eyed Jack pressing against my leg. I close my eyes and turn my head as he slides one hand lower to spread my knees apart, my entire body shivering at his touch. I don't resist because I've never resisted and soon he's onto me and into me, driving me deep into the mattress with his weight.

He pulls his hips back, then thrusts forward.
Again.
And again.
And I scream, and I wake, and my lover gathers me into her arms. She gently strokes my nearly-white hair and tries to kiss away the tears filling the corners of my eyes. Despite her love, she provides little comfort as I lay naked in a pool of sweat and menstrual blood

Michael Bracken

and realize that my long-dead father still casts his shadow over my bed.

A Thigh for a Thigh

Killing Johnny Dickenson wasn't hard — two well-placed slugs from my snub-nosed .357 took care of that. What *was* hard was deciding what to do with his body. After all, he weighed almost five hundred pounds and we couldn't very well stuff him under the hatch of my Escort and haul him off to the city dump.

"You've got the money, Paul," Sandy said nervously. "Let's just leave him." Sandy was the well-built redhead I'd been living with for nearly two years. "This place gives me the creeps."

I fondled the thick wad of bills in my jacket pocket and started to protest. "Somebody will find him here."

Sandy nervously shifted her weight from one foot to the other, her ample breasts subtly shifting position each time she moved, making me so horny I wanted her right there. "So what if they do? They can't trace the gun, can they?"

Michael Bracken

I admitted the police probably couldn't trace the revolver back to me. I'd stolen it before I met Sandy and I'd never used it before I put two slugs into Dickenson's jelly belly.

"Let's ditch the gun someplace and leave him there." Sandy motioned at Dickenson's body. He still sat at the battered wooden table, half a bucket of uneaten chicken before him. He'd slumped forward a bit, his thick chins resting on his chest. Even the blasts from the snubbie had failed to knock him from his chair, and I was sure that I couldn't move him even if I knew what to do with him.

I didn't have time to argue with Sandy, so we left Dickenson sitting in his kitchen as we rushed out of the tar paper shack. Even though Dickenson's shack was far from the edge of town, there was always the possibility that someone walking through the woods had heard the shots.

Once we were safely in the car and I was driving quickly away from Dickenson's shack, Sandy said, "I wonder what he meant when he said he'd get even with you."

"That was a bluff," I told her without taking my eyes from the road. "There was nothing the fat bastard could do but threaten me," I explained with a laugh. "And it didn't work, either, 'cause we got the money and he kissed his fat ass good-bye."

Sandy snuggled against me, her heavy breasts pressing against my arm. "How much did we get?"

With my left hand I pulled the wad of bills from the pocket of my loose blue jacket and tossed it into her lap. "Count it and see."

Sandy pulled off the rubber band and uncurled the bills. Then she peeled them one at a time from the wad. "Fifty, one hundred, one fifty...." She stopped counting at four thousand two hundred and fifty.

Canvas Bleeding

I whistled softly. It was the biggest haul I'd ever made.

Looking over at me in the darkness of the car, Sandy said, "I didn't know he'd have so much."

"I told you," I told her again. "Every Friday he waddled into the bank and handed the teller a fistful of ones and fives and left with a fifty."

I first noticed Dickenson the week after Thanksgiving when I was cashing my paycheck. He'd waddled into line just ahead of me, but I didn't pay much attention until two weeks later when I saw him leaving the bank with another fifty in his hand.

Off-and-on through the winter I ran into him at the bank. Finally one Friday I followed him from the bank to Stoney's where he stopped for two pitchers of draft beer. When he finished the second one, he climbed into his pickup and drove straight home.

"How about the river?" Sandy's question broke the silence in the car and interrupted my thoughts. "We could stop on one of the bridges and throw the gun over. They'll never find it down there."

I turned left at the main road to take the long way around into town. "Okay," I said. "Empty it first, then wipe off our prints."

Sandy carefully retrieved the revolver from its position between the two front seats, then opened it up to remove the four live rounds and two empty shells. Fifteen minutes later the revolver went sailing as far over the bridge's railing as I could throw it. The gun quickly sank from view. The two empty shells and the live rounds followed it a moment later.

"How about a steak dinner?" Sandy asked as she rolled down her window and let the cool wind whip her long red hair back around the headrest.

"Not tonight," I told her. "We can't be spending these fifties in town or somebody will know we stole

Michael Bracken

them." When I glanced over at her, she looked as if she was about to pout, so I added, "But tomorrow night we can dress up fancy and go to that place over in O'Shea. How about that?"

Saturday morning Sandy shook me awake and tossed the morning newspaper on the bed beside me. "They found him last night," she said. "When he didn't show up at the bank, one of the tellers got worried and called the cops."

I sat up and swore. Dickenson had only been dead since Wednesday. I hadn't thought about the tellers at the bank expecting him.

"It's okay," Sandy continued. "The paper says they've got no suspects and no motive."

Most of the wad of bills was in a shoe box in the bedroom closet. We had been careful not to spend the fifties in town where people knew us and knew I didn't earn enough to be flashing that kind of money.

I scanned the newspaper and started laughing. They'd had to use a crane to remove Dickenson's body from his kitchen. I finished reading the article and was relieved to see that nothing in the story implicated us.

After tossing the paper across the bed onto the hardwood floor, I pulled Sandy down to the mattress. "We're in the clear," I said with a laugh. "Nobody really liked the fat slob anyhow. It's not like he was the mayor or somebody."

I was naked under the cool sheets and I contemplated the nearness of Sandy's warm body. I reached for her, pulled her close, and twenty minutes later we lay side-by-side, basking in the warm afterglow of our coupling.

Canvas Bleeding

After a moment of silence, Sandy asked, "Are you gaining weight?"

"You say that every time," I told her. "Except when you're on top."

She laughed, and then we did it again — with her on top.

*F*or all of the next week we went about our business as if nothing had changed. By the following Friday when I cashed my check at the bank, the newspaper had dropped the story and word around Stoney's had it that Sheriff Ballany's office was planning to let the investigation fade into obscurity because it wasn't politically expedient to waste the taxpayers' money on a dead deadbeat.

Saturday I took Sandy into the city on a whirlwind tour of the best clothing stores in the downtown area. We found her a new dress, a trio of blouses and a pair of designer jeans that hugged her hips for full esthetic value. We stuffed all the packages into the back of my car and considered our next purchase.

"What about you?" Sandy asked. "We haven't gotten anything for you yet."

"That's okay," I told her. "You're more important." I'd knocked over a few gas stations and a liquor store since meeting her, but I'd never had the opportunity to spend so much money on her all at once.

"But we could get you that new suit you wanted," she said. "You've complained since we went to dinner a week-ago Thursday. We've still got a lot left. Come on." She took me by the hand and led me out of the parking garage and into a fancy men's shop where we eyed a rack of blue pin-stripes until a small man with fly-away white hair came to help us.

115

Michael Bracken

He asked my measurements, then pulled a suit from the rack and ushered me into a fitting room. After pulling the suit on, I stepped through the door to where Sandy and the little guy were standing.

"No, no, no," he said, shaking his head. Wisps of hair waved about. "That doesn't fit at all." He pulled a worn tape measure from his pants pocket and began sizing me up. "I thought you said you wore a thirty-four waist," he said as he removed the tape from around my stomach. "You're a thirty-eight."

I shrugged. "So I'm a thirty-eight. What's the difference?"

"The fit," he insisted, "is the difference." He picked another suit from the rack, exchanged jackets with a third suit and handed the combination to me. "Try this."

When I stepped from the fitting room a second time, he reached for the vest to straighten it. "There, now, that's how it's supposed to look. The vest and the jacket look fine. With this shirt and tie," he held them up to the suit for Sandy to see, "and a little work on that inseam, it'll look just fine."

I stared at myself in the mirror. It had been a long time since I'd worn a suit that fit properly. Still, I was looking at more cloth than I was used to. I turned to Sandy and asked, "What do you think?"

"Dashing," she said. "Maybe you should buy two."

The little man beamed.

"No." I shook my head. "I don't think so. One's enough."

After I returned to my street clothes and handed the suit back to the little man, I counted out seven fifties and laid them on the counter. He tucked them into the cash register, then pulled out a pair of tens and a handful of change for me.

"The suit will be ready to pick up in an hour," he

said. "Our tailor works until five today."

As we left the store, I turned to Sandy. "How about lunch?"

She threaded her arm in mine and led me through the crowd toward a small street-level café.

I used the last fifty two months later to buy a battered .38 Special from a long-time friend in the city. On the way home I knocked over a mom-and-pop grocery for a quick two hundred and stopped for a super deluxe pizza to take back to the apartment.

"Dinner's on," I said as I pushed the apartment door open with my foot.

Sandy looked up from her position on the couch. She was wearing a T-shirt and shorts. "Did you get pepperoni?"

"And extra mushrooms," I said as I placed the greasy box on the kitchen table. "Just like you wanted."

She turned off the television and joined me in the kitchen. "You want a beer?"

I nodded and opened the cardboard pizza box. Steam escaped and I deeply breathed in the aroma of the cheese and pepperoni. I scooped out the first slice of pizza with one hand and took an open beer can from Sandy with the other hand. My mouth full of hot cheese, I said, "Antonio's only gets better, doesn't it?"

Sandy eased her own slice of pizza from the box as she took the chair across the table from me. "It's good," she admitted. "But this is the third time this week you've stopped at Antonio's." With her free hand she pointed at my fleshy abdomen. "It's starting to show."

I looked down at the flab overhanging my wide

Michael Bracken

leather belt. "So? When things are going good, we eat good. When they aren't, then we don't eat so good."

She took a swallow from her beer as I attacked my second slice of pizza. I'd had an insatiable taste for pasta all week and the pizza was barely managing to take the edge off my hunger.

I pulled a wad of crumpled bills from my pocket and dropped them on the table next to the greasy pizza box. "I got another couple of hundred today," I said. "But I had to spend fifty for this." I pulled the .38 Special from the other pocket of my jacket.

Scooping up the bills with one hand, Sandy said, "I'll go shopping tomorrow. We're almost out of bread and beer."

Finally, as hungry as I was for the pizza, I knew I wanted Sandy even more. I pushed the pizza box aside and reached across the table to take one of Sandy's hands in mine.

*T*wo weeks later I returned to the apartment with some bad news. "Blume laid me off. His nephew's coming in from Chicago to attend the university over in Connorsville. Blume said the kid's going to be living with them and that he could do all of my chores."

Sandy swore. "What now?"

"Well, I've got almost a thou in the bank 'cause you made me save part of my check each week. That ought to get us by for a couple of months if we're careful."

"Then what, Paul?" she demanded. "Do we go back to the way it used to be? Scraping for every penny, clawing for every nickel?"

"I could knock over a gas station next week," I suggested.

Canvas Bleeding

"That's nickel-and-dime stuff, and you know it."

"I'll think of something," I said.

"You'd better, Paul, 'cause I don't want to go back to the way it used to be." She turned on her heel, stomped into the bedroom, and slammed the door.

Left alone in the living room, I glanced in the mirror above the couch and saw my reflection staring back at me. I looked tired, with dark bags hanging under my eyes and hard lines already forming around the edges of my mouth and the corners of my eyes. In the dim light, a shadow looked like a second chin. I brushed a hand through my wavy brown hair, then went to the kitchen in search of the revolver.

I found the .38 in the cupboard over the sink and I tried to tuck it into my waistband. It wouldn't fit comfortably so I shoved it in my jacket pocket and struggled to zip the blue jacket up over my abdomen. Then I headed down the stairs to my car.

I drove around most of the night, but I never saw any opportunities for quick money.

*T*wo and a half recessionary months later I still hadn't found a steady job to replace the one I'd lost at the motel, and I'd only managed to bring home eighty bucks from knocking over a self-serve gas station over on the edge of Connersville. Sandy became extra bitchy when the savings ran out.

After picking up dinner, I walked slowly back to the apartment with a bucket of chicken under my arm. I was walking with my head hanging down when I spotted a five dollar bill on the sidewalk, blown up against the brick wall of the pharmacy. I glanced around, saw that no one was watching me, then stooped to retrieve the Scotch-taped bill. It was amazing how much money

Michael Bracken

was lost on the street and I was surprised to realize I'd been finding quite a bit of it recently.

I tucked the five into my pocket and slowly walked the rest of the way back to the apartment building, then I huffed my way up the rickety wooden steps. When I opened the apartment door, I found Sandy standing by the couch trying to close her suitcase.

"What are you doing?" I demanded. I slammed the door closed and dropped the bucket of chicken on the end table.

"I'm leaving, Paul." She finally snapped the first lock closed.

"Why?"

"I'm sick of you." She snapped the other lock closed.

"Is it because of the money?" I asked. I knew where I might be able to get more: I'd seen the baker packing quite a bundle just that morning when I'd stopped in for a pair of éclairs.

"It isn't the money," she said. "It's you. I can't understand the way you've become."

"What? What's wrong with me?" I didn't understand.

"Don't you care about yourself anymore?" She hefted the suitcase in both hands and headed out the door. I wasn't going to let her leave so easily.

"Get out of my way," she demanded, her face growing red with anger. She pushed me aside, her thin fingers sinking into the soft flesh of my upper arm. Her red hair bounced behind her as she forced the door open. "You're a fat slob, Paul. You weren't like that when I first met you. You used to take care of yourself. You used to go down to the Y and lift weights."

Sandy slammed the door and I heard her tromp down the stairway to her Pinto.

I took a deep breath and felt my trousers tighten around my waist. I glanced in the mirror over the couch and realized I couldn't stand far enough back

Canvas Bleeding

for my entire girth to fit into the reflective glass. I sighed, then reached into my pocket and pulled out a fistful of crumpled bills and change. I counted out fifty dollars and looked at the calendar. It was Friday.

I decided I'd finish the bucket of chicken first, then I would waddle down to the bank and exchange the pile of bills for a fifty. Fifties were so much easier to keep track of.

To Sleep, Perchance to Die

*T*he last pill, the pill that made his hands shake and his legs twitch, he swallowed dry, with only his spittle to wash it down.

Nigel MacDonald sat waiting, silent in the darkened room. Within minutes the pill began to take effect. He stood, walked from one end of the room to the other, then back again. He turned on one lamp, then another. Soon the room flooded with light. This was the last night, the last pill, the last chance.

Desmond had promised him death, had forbid him sleep, had given him a promise. The promise was fear. Back across the room he walked, past thick curtains carelessly closed against the night, past heavy wooden

Michael Bracken

furniture created long before his birth, past dusty portraits of ancestors long dead.

The week had crept by despite the pills, perhaps because of them. He hadn't slept, hadn't dared to sleep. Alone in the house, he had spent the time pacing between the rooms, had climbed both flights of stairs more times than he dared count, and had descended them just as often. By now he knew the house, knew it even better than he had as a small child hiding from his grandfather in one of their endless games of hide-and-seek. Every nook and cranny, every dusty table, every cobweb caught in every corner was indelibly etched into his memory. And it didn't stop the pacing. It didn't stop the relentless pursuit of nothing.

Desmond would be returning soon. Nigel knew that. As soon as the effect of last pill finally wore off, Desmond would return.

Desmond — a man who had frightened him as a child and who he'd rarely spoken to as an adult — was a man who made promises and kept them.

Nigel's hand shook. He tried to light a cigarette, his hand shaking so violently three matches went out before he finally pulled in a long drag of smoke.

As he walked, the ashes fell from the cigarette onto the hardwood floor. He didn't care. It wouldn't be long until he would be beyond caring for anything or anyone.

The night grandfather died, Desmond visited. At first he tried to laugh off Desmond's warnings, tried to laugh off Desmond's prediction. But he couldn't. He knew only too well what Desmond could do.

After all, it was he who had asked Desmond to care for grandfather. It was he who had asked for grandfather's death. And Desmond had accommodated his wishes.

"But it was your grandfather's last wish that you be

cared for accordingly," Desmond told him that night. "He wanted you to think about it before you died. And you will. Because when you fall asleep, I'll come for you."

"I won't sleep," he'd said, and so he had found the amphetamines.

He had taken them from Grandfather's medicine cabinet, had examined them, and had slid them into his jacket pocket. At first, avoiding sleep was easy. Pacing, strong black coffee, a pair of No-Doze he found in his grandfather's kitchen cabinet. But as the morning came, his eyelids grew heavy. He'd taken the first pill with coffee and the second with juice. He'd begun to shake, his walking became faster, his movements spasmodic.

The bags under his eyes turned deep shades of purple, his fingertips yellowed from constant cigarette smoking. He stopped his daily showers, ceased changing his clothes. Now he smelled poorly; his clothes, coffee-stained and wrinkled, were sweat-glued to his gaunt frame; his hair, thick and greasy, hung limply down onto his collar.

The grandfather clock in the foyer clanged midnight. He continued walking. By two, he'd slowed a bit, his hands were a touch steadier, his legs moved without twitching. He drank more black coffee, cold this time. He struck his last match, lit his last cigarette, fumbled with an ashtray that finally dropped to the floor.

By four-thirty he was sitting again, resting in the chair where he'd so often sat on his grandfather's lap listening to his grandfather's stories of the Orient and India, his grandfather's stories about Desmond.

"I brought him back with me," grandfather liked to say. "He'd been a good manservant in Bombay. But I had to turn him out."

Michael Bracken

He'd always asked his grandfather why and his grandfather always shrugged his shoulders.

"Just not cut out for life in polite society, I suppose. The work he did for me when I was with Her Majesty's Secret Service just isn't appropriate here at home."

"But you allowed him to do those things in Bombay, didn't you grandfather?"

"Of course I did. He was around his own chaps then, but we just can't condone that kind of activity here."

Then grandfather would change the subject, tell about his perilous journey into Tibet, or his stopovers in the Middle East. Desmond stories grew farther and farther apart as Nigel grew older. Grandfather's wealth continued to grow, but his own efforts in the marketplace were doomed to failure. First one business venture, then another, failed. He was a poor manager of money and a poor manager of people.

For years grandfather's death had been imminent and, as his only heir, Nigel had waited — patiently at first, then with growing impatience. The old man had clung to life in that tiny bed in the west wing, so Nigel had gone to Desmond and Desmond had performed the contracted service. Now his grandfather was gone, buried in a family plot just south of town.

Desmond had performed that job for a substantial cash advance; the job he would soon perform for Nigel's grandfather he'd do out of respect and loyalty.

So Nigel sat alone in the house, the last cigarette burned down to the filter, the last cup of coffee sucked down to the dregs, the effect of the last pill finally wearing away.

A ray of early morning sunlight sliced through a gap in the curtains, bisecting his face with its brilliance. Nigel didn't notice. After days of pacing, after days spent contemplating his grandfather's wealth and his grandfather's death, he finally slept, slumped over in

Canvas Bleeding

his grandfather's chair.
 Desmond would soon arrive.

Voices

*J*oe stared at the crumpled twenty dollar bill gripped tightly in his grease-stained right fist. It was all that stood between him and starvation and the wind threatened to yank it away.

"Psst, Buddy!"

Joe looked up but saw no one.

"Over here. In the alley."

Joe turned toward the voice, but still couldn't see who had spoken.

"I'm back here."

"Leave me alone," Joe muttered. He began shuffling forward.

"Don't go," said the voice. "I want to talk to you."

Joe stopped.

"Just for a minute."

"About what?"

"Your future."

"I don't have a future." He shuffled away from the alley and didn't hear the voice again until three days later when all the money that remained now jingled in his pants pocket. When the voice called to him, Joe asked, "What now?"

"Looking for work?"

"For a year and a half."

"Girlfriend?"

"Last one left me when I lost my job at the plant."

"House?"

"I had a nice apartment," Joe said. "Now I live in my car."

"Nice car?"

"It was."

"I can get you a job, a house, a new car."

"How's that?"

"So you're ready to listen now?"

"Got nothing else to do." Joe stopped in the middle of the sidewalk to concentrate on the conversation and he didn't notice that everyone stepped carefully around him, always staying well outside of his reach.

"Check your pocket."

"Which one?"

"Right front."

Joe reached into his pants pocket and removed a dozen neatly-folded twenty dollar bills held together by a gold money clip shaped like a dollar sign. He examined each bill carefully, assuring himself that none were counterfeit. "Nice."

"There's more where that came from."

"What do I have to do for it?"

"Check into a room for the night. Shower. Shave. Clean yourself up."

"That's all?"

"To start."

Joe finally found a room at a transient hotel on Fifth, near the square, and paid a week's rent in advance. He bought shampoo, soap, and a disposable razor at a quick shop around the corner from the hotel. Then he cleaned up as best he could while standing in a cracked porcelain tub under the lukewarm dribble of water emanating from the shower head. He never noticed the thin river of blood swirling around his callused feet and down the drain.

After he toweled himself dry, Joe pulled on his only suit, a charcoal grey pinstripe he'd once worn to his father's funeral. It had been rolled up inside a plastic bag in the trunk of his car and smelled faintly of mildew and oil. After he'd fastened his blue paisley tie and straightened the Windsor knot, Joe stood in the middle of the room and asked, "Now what?"

He received no response from the voice. Instead, Joe's stomach growled. His last meal had been breakfast the day before — half a bran muffin and tepid coffee drunk from a Styrofoam cup imprinted with Cinnamon lipstick. He carefully counted the money remaining in his new money clip, then made his way to a chrome and porcelain diner two blocks from the hotel. He slipped into the first empty booth.

The lone waitress approached, her wilted white uniform and powder blue apron stained with the remains of hundreds of meals, her white off-brand tennis shoes squeaking on the linoleum as she hurried toward him.

He ordered without consulting the menu. Butt steak, rare; baked potato with butter, sour cream, and chives; broccoli smothered in cheese; and coffee. When his dinner arrived, Joe lingered over every bite.

After he'd eaten, Joe sipped his final cup of coffee while he studied the neatly printed bill the waitress had slipped under his salt shaker. He thought about it for a long time, then left her a two dollar tip.

He spent half the night sweating on the toilet bowel, his bowels cramping from the food he'd savored, his body unprepared for it.

He spent the next morning at a coin-operated Laun-

Michael Bracken

dromat, watching over his single load of clothes. That afternoon, he dropped his suit off at a dry cleaner, then had a palsied barber remove most of his greying shoulder-length brown hair.

*T*he money only lasted two more days, and the afternoon before his next week's rent was due at the hotel, Joe stood on the corner of Third and Manson reading a *Wall Street Journal* he'd retrieved from a trash barrel, his pockets empty.

"What time is it?"

"I'm not sure."

"Look at your left wrist."

Joe glanced up and discovered that the group of people he'd been standing with had already moved across the street ahead of him when the light changed. He pushed back his jacket sleeve and stared at the gold Rolex on his wrist. He whistled. "Nice."

"That's not all."

"What else?"

A young blonde woman in a severely cut red business suit and white running shoes stepped away from him.

"Inside jacket pocket."

Joe reached inside his jacket and retrieved a slim eelskin wallet containing $318. He counted the money twice.

*W*ithin a month, he opened a checking account, depositing $639 in cash.

"Nice feeling, isn't it?" asked the voice as he walked toward home.

Canvas Bleeding

"What?"

"Having money in the bank."

Joe shrugged. During the next few weeks, he began to feel even better as the two automatic teller machine cards in his wallet allowed him to withdraw $2,020 before they refused him further access to the accounts. He then charged $918.47 worth of clothing to an American Express card and used a MasterCard for $167.52 worth of shoes.

He joined a gym and began working out regularly. He lay in a tanning bed three times a week and his pallid complexion darkened to a healthy tan.

He stopped shuffling when he walked and he no longer looked away when people glanced at him. He even managed to pick up a petite brunette at a fern bar and take her back to his room one evening.

When she woke the next morning and realized he had brought her to a run-down room in a transient hotel, she cursed him. Joe didn't argue as she pulled on her clothes, and he watched as she slammed the door open and stalked down the hall.

Joe knew he needed a better place to live.

*T*he cellular phone in his briefcase rang and Joe reached inside to answer. The voice on the other end divulged inside information about a local electronics company.

Joe stopped at a corner kiosk and bought a local paper. He glanced at the front page headlines, skipping over the political news, the economic news, and the fifth murder in as many weeks. He flipped back to the financial section and scanned the stock listings until he found the electronics company the caller had mentioned.

He walked into a stock broker's office an hour later, opened an account in his own name and bought one hundred shares. A week later, he sold his stock for eight times what he'd paid. After paying the broker's fee, he had enough left over to press his suit and buy a Mercedes 350SL.

"*I* have a house for you."

"Yeah?" Joe had moved from the transient hotel to an executive suite in a posh hotel, but the monthly rent was killing him.

"In the 'burbs."

Joe reached into his pocket and retrieved an unfamiliar key ring. The voice gave him directions and later that afternoon he cleaned everything out of the executive suite and drove to his new home.

"Nice," he said as he stood in the driveway admiring the split-level and the well-manicured yard. Off in the distance he could hear children playing and dogs barking.

"And it's already furnished," said the voice. "Hope you like it."

Joe used one of the keys to open the front door, then strolled through the house. He examined the living room, dining room, kitchen, and all three bedrooms, but didn't really feel at home until he found a fully-stocked bar and a big-screen television in the den.

He used the remote control to bring the television to life and then flipped through the channels until a bleached-blonde anchorwoman caught his attention halfway through a story about another mugging-murder.

Canvas Bleeding

"The city just isn't safe anymore," Joe said, but the voice didn't respond.

Joe spoke to his broker, buying and selling stock using the tips he continued to get through his cellular phone. His trips into the city had stopped and he'd begun settling into a quiet suburban lifestyle, everything the voice had promised him.

Then one afternoon Joe answered a knock on his door, pulling the door open to reveal a pair of plainclothes police officers, their battered leather wallets open to display their badges. The two cops pushed their way into Joe's house.

"You're under arrest," said one of the cops, a burly Italian with bushy black hair and an oft-broken nose.

"It wasn't me," Joe said as he backed away.

"We found the Osgood family in the dumpster where you left them," said the other cop, a slim black man with delicate features and a three-inch scar along his jaw where a drug addict had caught him with the tip of a switchblade.

Joe screamed, "Tell them. Tell them who you are." He looked over his shoulder.

"The neighbors phoned and told us you were here."

The two officers slammed him against the wall, pressing his face against the plaster. They pulled his arms behind his back and snapped handcuffs tightly around his wrists, nearly eliminating circulation. One recited Joe's Miranda rights while the other examined the contents of Joe's pockets, including the wallet containing photos of someone else's wife and children.

"Tell them!" Joe screamed. "Help me!"

Thinking Joe might not be alone, both officers

Michael Bracken

searched every room, in every closet, under every bed. They found no one else in the house.

"Where the hell are you?" Joe pleaded as the two officers dragged him out the front door and down the walk to their unmarked car.

"*E*xcuse me."

Tucker looked up from his nearly empty bottle of Thunderbird and tried to focus on the source of the voice.

"I'd like to talk to you about your future."

Soul Man

"People die. That's all there is to it."

A conversation overheard in a dark, smoke-filled bar, the voices coming from two men straddling wooden stools at the far end of the bar. I strained to hear what came next.

"He swallowed a bullet!"

"It was his choice."

"The alternative?"

"Let's not discuss it here. Let's just say he chose the best option."

"For whom?"

I saw the shorter man shrug.

"It isn't what I wanted!"

The shorter man finished his beer, pushed his stool away from the bar, and stood. He held out his hand and his companion filled it with a thick white envelope. The envelope disappeared into a jacket pocket.

"Call me if you need anything else."

I watched the shorter man's reflection in the mirror behind the bar and I smiled as he passed behind me.

Michael Bracken

I waited a full minute, then slipped from my stool and moved to stand next to the one man remaining from the pair.

He finished his drink — a bourbon and water, I think — then glanced up at me, his pale grey eyes clouded with indecision.

"I can help you, Barney," I said.

He fixed his gaze on me. "Who are you?"

"A friend," I said. "At least, I could be."

"The friends I got —" he began.

"— you don't need enemies," I finished.

"Pull up a stool, mister," he said, "and tell me how you can help me."

Barney motioned the bartender over and had his drink refilled.

"The gentleman who just left," I said, "didn't have your best interests at heart."

"That's for damn sure," Barney said. He took a sip from his drink. "So why should I believe that you do?"

"Because you have nothing to lose and I have nothing to gain."

"How's that?" Barney slugged back half his drink while he waited for my answer.

"You've been fucking your partner's wife for nearly a year now, and skimming money for twice as long," I said. "Then you decided you wanted him out of the picture."

"I wanted him gone, not dead," Barney said.

"Still, his insurance will pay off quite handsomely. A million to the business, another half-mil to the distraught widow. And all it cost you was ten large to the gentleman I saw you with earlier."

Barney blanched. I had nailed everything. A moment later, his eyes narrowed to slits. "What do you want?"

"Everything."

Barney stared at me. "Or you'll go to the police?"

"I'd never do that," I said. "You've had a good life. Money, fast cars, cheap women. Everything you ever wanted. Is it everything you expected?"

"I thought so." Barney finished his drink. "Until now. I feel dirty, like I've just sold my soul to the devil."

I reached into Barney's chest and squeezed his heart between my fingers, watching his eyes as the realization of his impending death washed over him. Barney didn't realize it, but he'd sold his soul long before I ever arrived.

I just came to collect.

I'm the Soul Man.

What Little Girls Are Made Of

Dead again, and Mavis had left me alone to deal with it.

After taking Glory to the woods, I scrubbed the walls and hosed down the floor. I stuffed the bed linens in the washer and threw her one-eyed teddy bear in the trash. She wouldn't need it anymore. They never lasted long, these girls. Not long at all.

When I finished, I turned off the room's single light, a naked bulb that hung on a single strand in the center of the room, then walked upstairs to the main part of the house. Mavis had returned with groceries, three paper sacks stuffed full of microwave dinners and fruit-flavored soda pop from the Mega Market on Stateline. I helped her unpack and put the groceries

Michael Bracken

away.

"She's gone," I said finally.

Mavis looked at me. "Already?"

I shrugged.

"What'd you do this time?"

"Nothing."

She stared hard at me, but I didn't say anything else.

"It's too soon for another," she finally said.

What could I say? "Okay."

"Maybe next week," she said.

"I'm hungry," I told her.

"I'll fix something."

Mavis microwaved a lasagna and we sat at the kitchen table to eat. I had a can of grape soda and she opened a bottle of Jack Daniel's for herself, pouring out a tumbler full.

Halfway through the meal, she said, "I'll go tomorrow. I saw a place — a new place." We'd stopped picking the girls up at the Mall of Memphis after they installed the guard towers, and Mavis disliked competing with the pimps at the bus station downtown. She upended the tumbler and drained the last of its contents in one long swallow. "I'm sure it'll be all right."

My fork tines scraped against my plate. I didn't make any other sound during the entire meal.

"It's over near the river," she said as she refilled her tumbler. "Under the highway."

The following night, I sat in the back of the panel van, hidden in the shadows, and listened through the

Canvas Bleeding

open windows. I could hear the hum of tires on Interstate 55 above us as Mavis spoke to a young blonde we'd spotted earlier.

"You look like you could use a hot meal," Mavis told the girl.

"What do I have to do for it?" the girl asked cautiously. She couldn't have been older than twelve or thirteen.

"Nothing," Mavis said. She wore a simple black shift with a long-sleeved white blouse beneath it and thick-soled black shoes. A heavy silver crucifix hung around her neck and she'd pulled her hair into a tight bun. "Just ride with me back to the shelter. We'll get you a hot meal, some clean clothes."

The girl hesitated.

"How long have you been out here?"

"A month," said the girl. "Almost two."

"That's a long time to be on your own."

I could not hear the girl's mumbled response.

"I'll bet your parents are worried about you," Mavis said.

"Could I call my Mom, tell her I'm okay?"

I knew Mavis would be smiling now. This was her favorite part, talking to the girls and convincing them to come with us. The first time had been easy, before Mavis knew the girls should all be strangers, when Mother was alive and Mavis had brought home a friend from high school. That was the day I stopped playing with Mavis.

"It's long distance."

"Sure," Mavis said. "Not a problem at all."

When Mavis pulled open the van door, I shrank even further into the darkness and pulled an old army blanket over myself. I'd used it to carry Glory to the woods and it still smelled of her.

"You like music?" Mavis asked as she turned on the

Michael Bracken

radio, quickly finding a station playing current hits.

They didn't talk much during the drive and I almost fell asleep under the warm blanket.

"Where are we?" the girl asked as we pulled into the drive of Mavis' two-story home. We lived southeast of the airport, less than a mile from the Mississippi border, nearly half a mile from our nearest neighbor. "This doesn't look like any shelter I ever saw."

The automatic garage door opened and Mavis pulled the van inside, quickly dousing the lights and silencing the engine.

"What are we doing here?"

I flipped the Army blanket off of myself and over the girl. She struggled, but I held her tightly in my arms while Mavis opened the door. Young and weak from hunger, the blonde was no match for me and I easily carried her through the house and into the basement. Mavis followed with the girl's black canvas knapsack.

Mavis stripped away the girl's clothes and I hosed her down with cold water. Goose bumps covered the girl's flesh and her nipples tightened.

Mavis found a half-used bottle of shampoo on the shelf and she threw it at the girl. "Wash your hair."

*L*ater, I peeled the magnetic signs off the van doors, the white and blue ones advertising The Memphis Shelter for Homeless Children. Then I burned the girl's clothes in the trash barrel out back, pausing only long enough to inhale the aroma from her panties before shoving them into the fire with her soiled jeans and her tattered red flannel shirt.

"There's no identification," Mavis said. The girl's knapsack lay on the kitchen table, its former contents spread out beside it — a half-dozen changes of underwear, none of them clean; a sweatshirt from a college three states away; an opened box of tampons; and a pair of dog-eared romance novels.

I drank a can of raspberry soda, then I went downstairs to the girls' room where the blonde waited. She lay on the bed, covered only by a thin sheet, her arms wrapped around a battered, one-eyed teddy bear.

"Where did you get that?" I demanded.

"I found it," the girl whispered. "On the bed."

I hadn't seen it when we'd shoved the girl into the room, and I took the bear away from her, throwing it behind me and through the opened doorway. Then I peeled back the thin sheet and looked down at her. She tried to cover herself and scoot away from me at the same time. She couldn't do it.

I grabbed her wrist and held her. Then I pulled her close.

She was older than Glory, more developed.

"Did you give this to the new girl?" I asked when I returned to the living room.

Mavis looked up from the television program she'd been watching, a British comedy on the PBS station. She saw the bear in my hand and shook her head.

"I threw it away after Glory left."

"I didn't give it to her," Mavis said.

I stared at her for a moment, then walked back through the kitchen and out into the back yard. Embers still glowed in the trash barrel and I shoved the one-eyed bear into the coals, poking the embers with a stick to bring them back to life.

Glory had cried that first night when I took the bear away from her and she hadn't stopped crying until

Michael Bracken

Mavis dug it out of the trash and returned it to her.

I waited until Mavis had gone to bed before creeping down the back stairs to the kitchen, and then down into the basement. She didn't like me to bother the girls too many times in one day. "Play nice," she always told me, "or don't play at all."

I unlocked the heavy door and pulled it open. Light behind me cast my shadow across the girl. I stepped to the middle of the room and pulled the chain for the light.

The blonde had fallen asleep and she held the teddy bear trapped in her crossed arms. It stared up at me, its one good eye following every move I made.

"I took that away from you!" I yelled as I jerked the bear from her arms. It smelled of smoke and patches of hair had been burned away.

The girl woke suddenly, her eyes wide with fright.

"Where did you get this?" I demanded, shoving the smoky bear in her face.

"Glory gave it to me." She'd whispered so low I barely heard her.

"Glory's gone," I said. "Gone! I made her gone!"

"Glory said she used to live here," the girl whispered. "Glory said —"

No longer in the mood to play, I stormed out of the girls' room, stopping only long enough to ensure that I securely locked the door before I stomped up the stairs to the kitchen. I laid the bear face-down on the cutting board where Mavis sometimes diced vegetables, then I dug the butcher knife from one of the kitchen drawers and hacked the bear into hundreds of fuzzy little pieces.

Canvas Bleeding

Mavis interrupted me, stopping me as I brought the knife down for the umpteenth time. She took the butcher knife from me and laid it in the sink. "Haven't you done enough?"

I stared down at all the bits of fuzz.

"Go on to bed," she insisted. "I'll clean this up."

*T*he next morning only a few bits of fuzz still clung to the cutting board and I avoided looking at them. I found freshly-baked cinnamon rolls on the counter and I ate two of them with my morning soda.

Mavis entered the kitchen through the back door. She wore her yellow gardening gloves and she pulled them off by tugging on the fingertips.

"I buried the bear," she said. "It won't be back."

"Where?"

"In the woods."

I ate another cinnamon roll and opened another cherry soda.

*M*avis and I had bricked all four of the basement windows closed so that no light entered and none escaped. When I flipped the wall switch for the basement light, nothing happened. I hesitated a moment, then carefully walked down the steps with only the light filtering in through the open kitchen door to guide me.

Illumination barely reached back to the girls' room, but I knew my way even in the dark. I carried the last two cinnamon rolls on a paper plate and I unbolted the door with my free hand. A dirty, unwashed odor

147

Michael Bracken

assaulted my nostrils as I pulled the door open, but it wouldn't be the first time one of the girls had soiled herself or the room. I stepped inside and reached blindly for the pull string on the light.

Something struck my arm, knocking the plate of cinnamon rolls to the floor. I felt as if I'd been hit with a baseball bat — a baseball bat with claws.

I scrambled backward, pushing the door closed and leaning against it as I snapped the bolt into place.

Something large hit the inside of the door and the door shuddered.

I screamed for Mavis as I ran across the basement and up the stairs. She met me in the kitchen.

My shirt sleeve had been shredded and I bled from four long cuts that started at my left shoulder and led to my elbow. The cuts weren't deep.

"You fall on the rake?" Mavis asked as she wetted a cloth and dabbed away the blood.

"It's the girl," I said. "She's got something in there with her."

I told Mavis about the broken light and about opening the girls' room in the dark. By the time I'd finished, the blood on my arm had been washed away.

"Get the shotgun," she said.

I hurried upstairs to Mavis' bedroom and pulled the double-barreled Remington from under her bed. I broke it open and checked to make sure both barrels had been loaded. By the time I made it all the way to the basement with the shotgun, Mavis had replaced the broken light bulb and she stood in the center of a pool of light.

"Let's see what the girl's got," Mavis said.

She crossed the basement, unfastened the bolt, and pulled the door open. From the darkness inside the girls' room came a large, hairy brown paw, four claws extended, and it swiped across Mavis' throat before she could scream, and then she couldn't scream at all. She fell to the floor, her hands clutching her throat, blood bubbling from the spot where her larynx should have been.

I didn't stop to think about it. I squeezed both triggers of the shotgun, the blast knocking me backward onto my ass, the sound confined in such a small place deafening me, the flash from the muzzle blinding me.

I didn't move until the police found me sometime later. By then the girl had vanished and Mavis had bled to death. Later, they asked me a lot of questions and I told them about all of the girls and about how it had all been Mavis' idea.

I didn't tell them about Glory's one-eyed bear.

I didn't tell them the last thing I remembered in the basement as they led me up the stairs was looking back into the girls' room and seeing that battered little bear laying on its side in the middle of the floor, its one good eye watching me.

Feeding Mary Ellen

Mary Ellen's breasts were albino zeppelins capped with pale areolas that remained nearly invisible until she became aroused. Then they darkened like a blushing woman's cheeks and her nipples tightened into twin soldiers, standing firm and erect and awaiting orders.

Right now Mary Ellen lay on her back, filling most of the Queen-sized bed and snoring lightly. The flower-patterned sheet covered her only to the waist and her massive mammaries had slipped to each side, filling her armpits with mounds of milky white flesh threaded with barely-visible spider webs of blue veins.

I stood in the doorway between the bedroom and the living room watching her for a moment before pulling on my leather jacket.

I met Barney and Steven outside the Meet Market, a local singles bar that had often proven ripe for the picking. They'd been waiting nearly fifteen minutes and clearly expressed their displeasure by suggesting I pull my watch out of my ass.

"She's hungry," I said.

Mary Ellen had once been a model, many years ago, strutting the runways of New York and Paris with other anorexic and bulimic young women before her carnal desire consumed her. She'd been known world-wide, had modeled for all the best designers, had graced the covers of all the fashion magazines, had even signed an exclusive cosmetics contract. The year Little Grace disappeared from the fashion world, Mary Ellen's weight ballooned, providing her with a brief but well-received tenure as a large-sized model.

Then she grew too large for even those assignments and my role as her manager slowly changed.

*O*n this night, Barney's charms worked best, and of the three of us only he escorted a young woman home. He took her to the other side of the duplex while Steven and I watched on the big screen TV in the living room.

A plump young blonde, with curly hair cascading to her shoulders, a round face, and slightly upturned nose, she quickly stripped out of her clothes when Barney led her into the bedroom. Then she was in his arms, her heavy breasts mashed flat against his chest, her hands gripping his ass, and her hungry lips eagerly seeking his.

They kissed long and hard, and then she sank to her knees on the bedroom carpet. Steven returned from the kitchen with a pair of longnecks just as the blonde buried her face in Barney's crotch.

Canvas Bleeding

We hadn't rigged the other side of the duplex for sound, but I could imagine Barney's groan of pleasure as the blonde easily accepted his entire length into her oral cavity.

We were surprised a minute later when she swallowed every drop.

"It's a shame," Steven said. "A woman can do that ... it's a shame."

I knew what he meant.

She stood and tried to kiss Barney but he turned his mouth aside at the last moment and her lips landed on his cheek.

He spun her around to face the camera hidden behind the dresser mirror, standing behind her and reaching around to take her breasts in his hands. He cupped one in each hand, brushing the balls of his thumbs against her fat nipples and they quickly stiffened. Then, he took her from behind, holding her waist as he thrust forward again and again and again.

The blonde watched him in the mirror and we watched both of them on the big screen television. He must have been driving into her pretty damned hard because we could hear the dresser banging against the other side of the wall.

We knew the moment the blonde came because we watched her face and saw her mouth open in a scream of pleasure.

Afterward, Barney offered her a drink, one that allowed her to doze comfortably and to feel no pain.

*W*hen she stood, which wasn't often, Mary Ellen's distended stomach hung to mid-shin like a pale apron, providing unintentional modesty. Her breasts hung

Michael Bracken

like bloated tether balls nearly to her waist.

I had no fear of Mary Ellen, having lain with her many times before and after the night Little Grace disappeared, when we first learned of Mary Ellen's desire.

I buried my face between her corpulent thighs, feeling the dark jungle of her pubic hair dank and musky against my nose, the fatty apron of her stomach soft against the back of my head. I pressed my lips against hers, tasting her desire. I felt Mary Ellen's deep intake of breath and the slight shift of her thighs as I pleasured her with my tongue.

Then she came and when she came Mary Ellen's body rolled in a tsunami of flesh that began at her pubic juncture and rolled upward and downward simultaneously. Then, reaching the ends of her, rolled back again to collide in the fatty apron covering my head.

Afterward, as she lay in the dark, Mary Ellen whispered, "Feed me."

After laying the plump young blonde next to Mary Ellen, we turned away, closing the door behind us as we returned to the living room. We found an old Vincent Price movie on one of the cable stations. Then Barney retrieved a six pack of longnecks from the refrigerator and we waited.

We had seen it all before, watching in fascination as Mary Ellen absorbed the smaller woman, becoming one with her. The first time had been accidental, two bulimic models away from home and sharing a bed in their first tentative lesbian encounter, lying in one another's arms after mutual orgasm.

I had walked into Mary Ellen's hotel room that day

unannounced, discovering her bloated body absorbing the last of Little Grace's right leg. I canceled the day's shoot, announced Mary Ellen's admission to a rehab center for weight disorders, and fended off police questions regarding Little Grace's disappearance.

Since then I had done everything to feed Mary Ellen's desire, caring for her when she could no longer care for herself, and preparing for her the orgy of flesh that she consummated and consumed with desire, Mary Ellen absorbing her fountain of youth until she became every woman with whom she had ever lain.

Something I Did with My Hands

On Christmas Eve there were no miracles in sight. Instead, Evan McLoed sat alone in his apartment and stared out the sliding glass doors down at the parking lot where the residents' cars — most of them still covered with a light dusting of snow from that morning's brief storm — were barely visible. In his left hand, Evan held a bottle of Jack Daniel's. Every so often he lifted it to pour two or three fingers of Tennessee pride into the tumbler he held in his right hand. Then he would raise the tumbler to his lips and empty it, letting the liquor cascade down the back of his throat.

Taped to the wall behind him were three Christmas cards — the one from his ex-wife containing a note

Michael Bracken

demanding the over-due child support, the one from his insurance agent reminding him that his policy would soon expire, and the one from his former employer mailed three days before he'd been laid off. He'd taped them up in a triangle, intending to tape all his cards to the wall in the shape of a Christmas tree. On the floor below the cards lay a brightly-wrapped Christmas gift, large enough and heavy enough to contain a bowling ball. The gift's red and white paper, green ribbon, and gold bow were the only splash of color in a living room drab with browns and beiges and wood-tones.

He'd found the package waiting for him in the lobby the previous evening after he'd spent the entire day at the unemployment office. It had been wrapped in plain brown paper and his name and address had been carefully penned in child-like block letters directly on the wrapping paper. There had been no return address.

Somewhere outside a car horn blared. Evan lifted the bottle to pour, then realized he'd emptied it with his last drink and he dropped the bottle to the floor. He stayed in the chair for almost an hour, staring at nothing in particular. When he finally pushed himself up and out of the chair, he stumbled into the kitchen and pulled open the cabinet doors looking for a second bottle he knew he wouldn't find.

Finally settling on a half-empty can of Pepsi he found in the refrigerator, Evan carried the can back to the chair, poured its contents into his tumbler, and drank. The Pepsi had gone flat sometime the previous day but he didn't notice.

Evan was still in the chair when he finally fell asleep. The empty tumbler slipped from his relaxed fingers and dropped quietly to the carpet.

He dreamed the dreams of the inebriated — formless, shapeless dreams that caused him to twitch and shud-

Canvas Bleeding

der and half-rise from the chair as if he were about to awake. Then he would fall back, pull his knees up almost to his chin and dream of the womb he could never return to, his son screaming for him to come out and play, his ex-wife screaming at him to go away.

"She doesn't love you, Daddy," his son said in the kaleidoscope of his dream. "Why doesn't she love you? I love you, Daddy."

He dreamed of the hours he'd spent in his workshop before he'd lost it, his son at his side, together creating things with their hands because hand-made is best-made.

At the end, his ex-wife screamed at him, called him names, insulted his manhood, but in the courtroom she'd been the perfect little housewife, well coached by a lawyer far more expensive than his own. Despite his best efforts, she'd been granted custody. Less than a year later, when he'd returned his son nine days after the beginning of a seven-day hunting trip during which Evan had taught his son how to gut a deer, two days after his ex-wife had notified the police and accused him of kidnapping, the court had denied him visitation rights. Then she'd taken his son and moved to California, refusing even to provide him with her unlisted telephone number.

The nightmares had come and gone as he'd missed his son's tenth, eleventh, and twelfth birthdays, and they'd gotten worse after he'd lost his job. The nightmares reminded him of everything he'd ever lost, of every missed opportunity.

When the first light of dawn assaulted him, Evan tried to turn away, to roll over and bury his head under a pillow, but he couldn't. In the bedroom, his alarm clock began its electronic whine. He reached out to slap it off but succeeded only in knocking the television's rabbit ears to the floor. He swung again for the

Michael Bracken

alarm clock in the next room. He gashed one of his knuckles on the television knobs and the pain roused him enough that he quit thrashing about.

He sat up, trying to shield his eyes from the morning sun with one hand while he sucked at the gashed knuckle on the other. Warm blood trickled over his tongue but he could barely taste it. Instead, his felt as if the inside of his mouth were a rotted tree stump, covered with moss and fungi. He pushed himself out of the chair with a groan and turned his back to the dawn's light. His stomach began a series of calisthenics and he lurched toward the bathroom.

On his way, Evan stumbled over the package, tearing open one corner of the wrapping paper as he kicked it with one of his black wingtips. Christmas morning had arrived despite his best efforts to obliterate it with bourbon, and after he heaved his gut nearly dry and wiped his forehead with a damp cloth, Evan returned to the living room to unwrap his only present.

He sat beside it on the beige carpet and ripped off the gold bow, slipped off the green ribbon, and tore away the red and white paper, ensuring that none of the wrapping material could ever be reused. Then he tore at the tape sealing the box, tearing his fingernails and cutting his left thumb on a brass staple. As he sucked his bleeding thumb, Even reached into the box and pulled out a black trash bag, sealed shut by a pair of twist ties.

The Christmas card attached to the bag had been handmade, the Christmas tree and its ornaments colored with blunt crayons, and the two people pictured beside the tree looked everything like a man and a boy. Evan opened the card and read the inscription, "I hope you like it, Daddy. It's something I did with my hands."

Evan set the card aside, untwisted both ties from the

Canvas Bleeding

plastic garbage bag, and almost threw up again when the smell escaped and assaulted his olfactory senses. He peeled away the plastic and a sudden assault of dry heaves forced him onto his hands and knees.

He scuttled away from his ex-wife's rotting head.

On Christmas day there were no miracles in sight, but Evan had received the best gift of all.

With Skin So Pale and Canvas Bleeding

*T*he Harley idled between Monk's legs, sending the familiar erotic tingle through his crotch and making his dick hard. The ride over from the house had been eventful only because a young blonde had nearly driven her Miata into a parked car when he'd roared up beside her. He slipped the kickstand down, cut the engine, and leaned the bike over to rest on the 'stand. Twelve other bikes were already lined up outside Crossbones.

He swung off the Harley, then strode across the cracked sidewalk and up the three steps into the bar.

Michael Bracken

Monk wore his sleeveless denim jacket and his black Jack Daniel's T-shirt stretched taut across his shoulders.

Bikers filled Crossbones. They wore grease-stained blue jeans, faded and frayed; sleeveless denim jackets or road-soiled leather jackets; T-shirts straining to encompass guts that spilled over wide leather belts. Large black wallets protruding from rear pockets had been chained to their belts. They had unkempt beards dusty from the road, long hair pulled back into pony-tails or held away from wary eyes with rolled bandannas tied around their heads. Cigarettes of tobacco and marijuana dangled from thick lips. Hardened fists engulfed longneck beers.

Many had scars. From accidents, from fights.

And tattoos. Every exposed arm had been covered with snakes and skulls and roses and daggers and the names of too many women.

The bitches — some beautiful, some not — strutted their stuff, their T-shirts too tight, their jeans too small. A few were topless or wore only unbuttoned sleeveless denim jackets. Monk had been with at least half of them; the others were too skanky even for him.

Monk straddled a bar stool, ordered a longneck, and stared into the mirror while he drank. A few minutes later, he watched the reflection of Gimp limping into the bar, a wooden cane carrying most of his weight in place of the left leg he'd shattered in a right-of-way dispute with a Lincoln Town Car seven years earlier.

A snake coiled around Gimp's arm, then over his shoulder, the fangs biting into his neck and drawing blood. It writhed in the dim light of the bar and two of the bitches backed away as Gimp limped past them.

"Nice tat," Monk said when Gimp straddled the chrome and red vinyl stool beside him. "Son-of-a-bitch looks real."

"It's 3-D."

Canvas Bleeding

The other tattoos along Gimp's arms and back — the skulls and crossbones, the naked women with their unnaturally large breasts, the daggers and the swords — were nothing more than the work of color-blind beginners with tattoo-by-number kits. Whoever had etched the snake in Gimp's arm had been a Michelangelo of skin art.

"Who did it?" Monk asked. "I never seen his work before."

"This new guy," Gimp said. "On Fifth."

"Take me to him."

"I ain't had my beer yet," Gimp said. "Besides, he don't open till dark."

Monk ordered his friend a longneck and they drank until one of the skanky bitches took Gimp into the back room for an hour. By the time he returned to the stool beside Monk, the sun had set.

Gimp could still ride. After the accident the other bikers had rebuilt his mangled Electra Glide. When Gimp's leg finally came out of the cast, his bike was good as new and his new nickname firmly entrenched.

He led Monk to the new tattoo parlor on Fifth, a filthy place sandwiched between a leather shop and a used record store, both already closed for the night.

Monk examined three-dozen examples tacked on the wall and a photo album with nearly a hundred Polaroids crammed into it. All manner of snakes and daggers, every tattoo a representation of something sharp, pointed, able to draw blood, but none so real as the tattoo on Gimp's arm.

"You done this?" Monk asked, pointing to Gimp's new tat.

The tattooist nodded. So sickly pale, Monk could see the webbing of veins beneath the tattooist's translucent skin.

"How much?"

Michael Bracken

"It's a small price to pay," Gimp said.

Monk examined the tattooist. "How come you never done yourself?"

The tattooist shrugged.

"There ain't no mirrors," Monk said. "How'm I gonna see what you done?"

The tattooist finally spoke. "You'll know."

Monk slipped out of his sleeveless denim jacket and peeled off his sweat-stained T-shirt. Then he straddled the old barber's chair and leaned back until he lay nearly flat. When the tattooist offered him a shot of whiskey, Monk took two.

The tattooist started his needle and approached Monk. Monk jerked his arm away.

"Don't you need to be sketching something first?" Monk asked. "Put some marks on my arm so you know what you're doing?"

The tattooist silenced him. He began at Monk's left wrist and began working around his arm and upward. What began as a series of seemingly random black lines developed into the outline of a winged serpent stretching upward to bite Monk's jugular. Then, colors filled in, the serpent gained texture, depth, dimension.

"The sun'll be up soon," Gimp said. He'd been pacing.

"I'm almost finished."

Finally, the tattoo needle stopped whining.

Monk looked down at his arm. The tattoo lacked the three-dimensional quality of Gimp's. "You ain't done!"

"One last thing."

For the finishing touch, the tattooist leaned over and sank two needle-sharp canine teeth into Monk's jugular. Monk's eyes went wide and he struggled. Despite his frail appearance, the tattooist easily held Monk in place as he drank.

Canvas Bleeding

When Monk's dragon came to life, the tattooist pulled his face away from Monk's neck and there, at the exact spot where the winged serpent's two teeth were embedded in Monk's neck, he'd left the canvas bleeding.

Fat Chicks Must Die

Constance Puge had been a corpulent woman, with heavy breasts like twin tether balls hanging from her chest and thighs like Sequoia stumps that tapered down to ankles so dainty they should have snapped when she walked.

"Jesus," Roderick said under his breath. "Couldn't you have asked her to climb into the pickup before you shot her?"

He strained to lift the dead woman's shoulders while I lifted her legs. Between us, we couldn't lift her ass off the ground.

"Now what do we do?" Roderick demanded. "We can't leave her here."

I released Puge's ankles and her legs fell with a thump that sent a cloud of dust billowing up toward my face.

"Should I have left her where she was?"

"No." Roderick violently shook his head. "No way."

Michael Bracken

When I'd found them, she'd been sitting naked on Roderick's face screaming, "Eat me, you little shit!"

What I could see of Roderick's face under her ample ass had been an odd color of blue and I knew he wasn't breathing. I ordered Puge to remove her bulk from on top of Roderick, even pulled out my revolver and pointed it straight at her to emphasize my sincerity, but she'd refused.

"I won't move until this little prick eats me."

That's when I shot her.

Once.

She died right there on top of Roderick, slowly falling forward until her face lay buried in his crotch. The change in her position was just enough so that Roderick could start breathing again, but it took me almost ten minutes to push her corpulent body off of him.

"I thought you liked fat chicks," I said as I hopped up onto the tailgate of my pickup and stared down at Puge.

"I used to," Roderick said, "until this." He mopped his forehead with a red bandanna he'd pulled from his hip pocket. "Think we can drag her out of here? Wrap some of that chain around her ankles, hook it over the trailer hitch?"

I imagined us dragging a quarter ton of woman along the dirt road toward town and I shook my head. "There's got to be a better way."

"Bury her."

"In this ground? It's sun-baked clay, hard as brick." I stared at Roderick. "Figure something out. You got us into this mess."

"Hey, butt-head," he said indignantly, "*I* didn't shoot her."

"I saved your life, you ungrateful prick."

Roderick glared at me for a moment, then the fight

slowly left him. "Yeah, maybe you did." He rummaged through the junk in the back of my pickup for about five minutes, then said, "Chainsaw."

"Chainsaw?" I said. "You know what kind of mess that'd make?"

Roderick looked at me, then at the chainsaw, and then at Puge's body. He reached for the half-filled gas can I kept with the chainsaw. "You got a match?"

*I*t took the rest of the afternoon to burn Puge's body, then scrape the remains into a leaf bag Roderick found in the bed of my pickup. By the time we'd finished, we both smelled something atrocious, but the only evidence that Puge had visited that spot was an oily stain on the sun-baked clay.

Satisfied with the result, we hoisted the leaf bag into the bed of the pickup and drove down to the reservoir. We found some heavy rocks, stuffed them into the leaf bag with Puge, then tied a knot in the bag and dropped the whole thing over the edge of the dam. The bag quickly sank out of sight.

"There now," Roderick said as we walked back to the truck. "That wasn't none too hard, was it?"

"What do we say when they come looking for her?"

"Not a thing," Roderick said. "Not a damn thing."

We both remained silent on the ride home. I'm not sure what thoughts occupied Roderick's mind, but I couldn't stop thinking about pulling the trigger. I'd meant to frighten Puge, not kill her. Just frighten her.

I dropped Roderick off at his place, a run-down

single-wide on a half-acre of land. He didn't say anything when he climbed out of my pickup and I didn't say anything either. I didn't even glance in my rearview because I didn't want to know if he went inside or if he stood on the hard-packed dirt of his front yard and watched as I drove away.

I stopped at Little Bubba's Package Liquors and bought a cold six-pack of Lone Star longnecks to keep me company. I drank the first in Little Bubba's parking lot and tossed the empty in the bed of my pickup next to the chainsaw and the empty gas can. I drank the next three while sitting on my couch cleaning my revolver and watching professional wrestling.

When wrestling ended, I stuffed the remaining longnecks in the fridge, wrapped the freshly cleaned and reloaded revolver in an oil rag and hid it under my bed, then took a long, hot shower that nearly washed away the smell of the day.

*T*he following morning found me draining the oil from a 4x4 at Junior's Garage, the only place in town for auto repair unless you took your car out to the new Wal-Mart by the highway.

"Nobody's seen that fat broad lives over on Maple," Junior said. "The sheriff was up here earlier asking around."

"Not since Sunday morning when she waddled home from church," Eddie Ray said as he wiped his hands on an oily rag. "Damn near shook the pictures off the wall when she walked by my place."

"They say inside every fat woman is a skinny woman screaming to get out," Junior said.

"Why's that?" I asked.

"That's 'cause the fat woman ate her."

Junior and Eddie Ray laughed their asses off over that one, but I turned my back on both of them and stuck my head under the 4x4's hood.

At noon I walked over to Eats, a diner just down the block from the garage, and overheard Molly the waitress and Pastor Duncan talking about Constance.

"The Holy Ghost certainly got up inside her last Sunday," Molly said as she leaned over the Formica counter top and flashed the Pastor the tops of her melons. "She was a amenin' and praise Jesusin' with the best of 'em."

"That's what bothers me," Pastor Duncan said. "I stopped by to visit her that very evening and she wasn't home. It's not like Miss Puge to miss a prayer visit like that."

I ate my cheeseburger and fries in silence, keeping my comments to myself lest anyone think I had an opinion about the disappearance of the town's biggest asset.

Talk of her disappearance occupied the back fence gossips all day and into the next. Everyone in town had an opinion about Constance Puge and her weight and many of the men rattled off variations of their favorite fat jokes.

*T*he jangling of the telephone woke me Tuesday night and I knocked the lamp off my night stand reaching for it.

"Yuh," I said. The inside of my mouth tasted like road tar and dog shit.

"Get over here!" Roderick shouted into my ear. I hadn't seen him or talked to him since Sunday afternoon. "Bring your gun!"

I scrambled out of bed, pulled on the same grease-stained jeans I'd worn the day before, found a Dallas

Michael Bracken

Cowboys T-shirt on top of my dresser, and hopped down the hallway pulling on my boots. I had to go back for my revolver when I realized I'd left it under my bed.

Fifteen minutes later I swung a hard left and pulled into Roderick's drive.

No light of any kind shone from inside his mobile home, not even the neon Budweiser sign in the kitchen that Roderick kept on twenty-four hours a day.

I stood on the brakes and my pickup slid to a halt in Roderick's front yard, kicking up a cloud of dust that I choked my way through as I scrambled out of the truck and across the yard to the single-wide's front door.

I pushed open the front door. "Roderick!"

When I heard no response, I tried the wall switch, flicking it up and down without result. I stepped into the living room and felt my way down the hall to the bedroom.

The room smelled of ejaculate and gasoline and I found Roderick laying on top of his bed, naked as the day he was born. He didn't respond when I called his name. I shook his shoulder without result. Then I took his wrist in my hand and felt for a pulse.

There was none.

I felt for the phone, found it, and brought it to my ear. There was no dial tone.

I shook Roderick again, felt again for a pulse, and then swore like a truck driver as I scrambled out of his mobile home and drove half a mile to a pay phone outside the Suds-and-Duds Washateria where I phoned the police.

I returned to Roderick's mobile home a few minutes later to find it engulfed in flames and I stood next to my truck watching it burn until the first police cruiser wheeled into the front yard next to me.

Canvas Bleeding

By the time the fire department responded, the mobile home had been reduced to its steel frame and some smoldering ashes.

I stood with one of the two police officers who had responded to my call, a portly, grey-haired sergeant who'd been on the force since I was in grade school. I told him about the phone call, but I didn't mention the loaded revolver in my pickup.

"What do you think frightened him?" Sergeant Callus asked.

I shrugged my shoulders and tried to avoid looking at my reflection in his mirrored sunglasses. "Roderick was never the kind to scare easy," I said.

"Hey, Sergeant," called the other officer, a pimply-faced young man who must have been barely a month out of the academy. He had his flashlight pointed at the hard-packed dirt near the front steps.

I followed the sergeant and we both looked down at the clear imprints of a woman's high-heeled shoes.

"Your buddy have a lady friend over tonight?" Sergeant Callus asked.

"Must have been a damn big woman," said the young cop, "to leave her footprints in dirt this hard-packed."

"He liked 'em big," I said. "Roderick always said the bigger the cushion, the better the pushin'."

"Hmph," said the sergeant. He pulled a notebook from his hip pocket and made a note with the stub end of a pencil.

Then the young cop asked, "You know that lady we been looking for, Sarge? She's a big woman, ain't she?"

Sergeant Callus scribbled in his notebook.

We spoke for another twenty minutes or so before Sergeant Callus sent me on home. I showered, washing the smoke from my hair, and then I popped open a longneck and settled onto the couch.

175

Michael Bracken

Roderick had called for my help, but I had been too late.

*T*here wasn't enough left of Roderick to autopsy and the sheriff took my word that Roderick had died before the fire consumed him. I didn't tell them about the thick smell of gasoline and sweat and ejaculate in his bedroom and they didn't ask me about the footprint in the dirt outside his front door. If I didn't know better, I could have guessed who had left it.

With two mysteries, the town was abuzz with gossip and rumor and I could not escape the constant chatter even at work.

"Took his own life, is what I heard," Junior said at the garage one morning a few days later. He already had a cold beer in his hand, his second of the day. "Ain't that right?"

I shrugged.

"You was there, wasn't you?"

"Less you killed him," Eddie Ray said. He looked up at me from under the hood of a 1968 Mustang. "You was the one found the body before it burned up."

"I was fixing to start on the Pastor's minivan," I said, trying to distance myself from Junior and Eddie Ray. "Leave me to get to it."

"You know something about it you ain't telling," Junior said. He took a healthy swallow from his beer. "Otherwise you'd stay here jaw bonin' with us about it."

I turned and walked outside to the pastor's minivan and I spent the rest of the day with my head buried deeply under the hoods of a series of cars.

After work that night I drove out to the dam and stared down into the dark water for a long time. I stood in the same place Roderick had stood when he heaved the rock-filled leaf bag over the side. Then I stopped at Little Bubba's Package Liquors for a six of longnecks, drove home, and drank myself to sleep without turning off the shadeless lamp on my dresser.

I awoke with a start. Constance Puge stood at the end of my bed, as naked as she'd been the Sunday afternoon I'd killed her. Her heavy breasts hung like over-filled water balloons from her chest and the fat of her stomach hung like a flesh apron down to her knees. She smelled of smoke and gasoline and dirty water and sex and sweat and I gagged.

"Eat me," she said. All of her chins flapped when she spoke and spittle flew from her thick lips.

"Jesus Fucking Christ!" I screamed, scrambling over the side of my bed and reaching under the mattress for my revolver. I pulled away the oily rag I kept wrapped around the gun and gripped it with both hands as I pointed it at her.

"Eat me," Constance said again as she stepped forward. Her butt brushed against my dresser, knocking the lamp to the floor.

"I killed you!" I screamed at the fat woman. I had killed her as dead as the deer head I had mounted in the living room. I saw a tendril of smoke curl up from the floor behind her as the carpet caught fire.

"Eat me, Billy. Eat me."

She stepped forward again and I squeezed the revolver's trigger until the hammer slammed down on spent shells. I continued squeezing until Constance knocked the gun from my hand, pushed me onto my back, and sat on my face.

I stuck at her with my fists, her doughy flesh absorbing each of my ineffective blows. I knew then what had happened to Roderick.

"Eat me," Constance said as her corpulent thighs slowly smothered me and the house burned down around us.

I opened my eyes and saw myself reflected in Sergeant Callus' mirrored sunglasses. Only I didn't really see myself.

"Everybody's been worried sick about you, Miss Puge," the sergeant said. He had his notebook in one hand, a pencil in the other.

I screamed.

"Just where have you been these past few days?"

"I got burned in a bad relationship," Constance said. A tiny smile pulled at the corners of her thick lips. "And I had to take a few days to straighten things out."

Sergeant Callus made a note. "That's all?"

I screamed again and again and again and no one ever heard me.

"You know how men are," Constance told the sergeant. "Sometimes they get under your skin."

Violent Eyes

I sat in a rented Ford, scanning the neighborhood. The weed-choked yards, the screen doors hanging crookedly on their hinges, the rusted automobiles propped on cinder blocks along the parking strip had attracted me because emotions always ran at the surface in people who lived on the edge.

My concentration skipped from house to house, mind to mind as I scanned down one side of the street and up the other. Within minutes I located a depressed housewife with a screaming baby and too many loads of laundry to do. She shook the kid, yelling at it. I felt her frustration. She hated the baby; hated the baby's father; hated the laundry she did for the neighbors.

I stopped scanning and focused. Then I twisted the emotion inside her, amplified the level of hatred past rationality, and felt adrenaline surge as she pounded the baby's face into the dirty plaster wall. Finally the baby ceased its relentless crying.

I pulled back slowly, savoring the last moments of contact. The adrenaline had begun to wash away, re-

Michael Bracken

placed by a sense of accomplishment; she did not yet comprehend what she had done.

"Mister?" A small hand shook my shoulder. "Are you okay, mister?"

I took a deep breath and opened my eyes. My vision blurred and my head hurt. I turned slowly. A boy in a faded blue T-shirt stared at me.

"Do you need help?"

"I'm okay." I licked my lips.

Hot, muggy weather gripped St. Louis. All four of the car's windows had been rolled down so the thin breeze could reach me while I scanned. It hadn't been enough: my back was plastered to the vinyl seat, the sweat-soaked fabric of my shirt sandwiched in between. Scanning and the heat had drained me.

"Are you sure?" the boy insisted. "You don't look so good."

I leaned forward and started the car. "I'm fine," I insisted. I dropped the car into gear and slowly pulled from the curb. Half a block behind me, seen only in my rear-view mirror, a pudgy young woman came screaming from one of the ramshackle bungalows. She carried something limp in her arms. The boy turned toward her. I turned on the radio.

At the hotel I changed clothes, leaving my shirt and my jeans in the shower to dry. Then I phoned room service, ordered a bottle of Jim Beam, and sat alone in the room steadying my nerves.

Scanning is physically demanding. Often I return disorientated, unsure of where I am. When possible, I give myself time to adjust. The boy had interrupted me, thrown off my concentration, and my hands had

Canvas Bleeding

shaken violently all the way to the hotel.

I savored the Jim Beam when it arrived. A frequent companion, it temporarily washed away the after-effects, drowned some of the memories.

I'd first noticed my ability to scan as a toddler. Standing close to certain people, I'd felt their emotions. I'd known when they were happy and when they were sad; I'd known when they were afraid and when they were courageous; I'd known when they were overcome by any emotion at all. But I didn't realize then that I was different. I didn't realize it until I reached thirteen. A bully who hated everyone and everything picked me for his punching bag. Too small to fight, too scared to run, I suffered his blows, but I also felt his hatred and wanted to know from where it came. I scanned, not realizing I was scanning, fine tuning into his mind because it was so close. I found the place inside where the hatred festered and I twisted it — twisted it like the volume control on a television set.

He turned away and ran blindly into the grill of an oncoming Edsel.

I watched, our contact broken when he'd stepped away, and then I fainted. I woke in my bed. The doctor encouraged my parents to keep me home until I recovered from the trauma of watching a friend die.

I began to experiment after that, entering minds at random. I tried for distance, length of stay, most number of minds visited in a short time. I entered specific minds, twisting emotions with the little bit of control I then had. When my grandmother died of cancer she was happier than she had ever been; when the next-door-neighbor boy dissected his mother's French poodle with a carving knife, he'd never been more vengeful.

As I grew older, my abilities increased, within the limitations I'd discovered as a teenager. I could enter a mind and twist the emotion I found, make it more intense or make it disappear. Then I stayed for the ride, seeing where it went, leaving when it finished. Before long, the rosy glow of love and the warm embrace of pleasure no longer provided excitement. I strove for the thrill of mainlining adrenaline or orgasm without end, the edge of humanity where animal instinct dominates.

I could never read minds, could not control someone, could not make him say or do what I desired. I could only twist his emotions and hang my shirts to dry afterward.

I stared at the glass in my hand, realized I'd drained it, and pushed myself out of the chair. I straightened my tie before leaving the hotel room, then headed to a sales meeting I had scheduled.

It took the rest of the afternoon to convince the president of a typesetting company to invest a quarter million dollars and bring his composing room equipment up to current industry standards. It didn't matter that what he bought would be obsolete the next day, what mattered was that I had his signature on a contract when I finally left the building.

When I had the chance, I scanned all the minds in a room before I entered, toning down the negative emotions and amplifying the positive ones. I didn't often have the chance: scanning with pin-point accuracy took too much effort, too much sweat, and too much concentration, to do well under the watchful eye of even the least efficient secretary. I'd tried once, early in my career, only to return from scanning to find myself lying on a reception room floor with two para-

Canvas Bleeding

medics hovering over me, preparing to take me to the hospital. After that I sometimes slipped into the men's room, found a stall, and did a quick blanket scan of everyone within a short range, twisting the positive emotions up to full volume, hoping I caught my target in the scan.

Since the sales meeting had gone well, I celebrated by treating myself to a lobster dinner, an adventure movie, and a quiet drink in the hotel bar before going up to my room for the night.

I stripped and lay in bed staring at the ceiling, seeing the whorls of paint and the tiny shadows they cast. I wasn't tired: the adrenaline rush of the afternoon, and the ego-boosting accomplishment of another signed contract, kept my mind racing. I took a deep breath, tried to concentrate, and finally began scanning the hotel. I whipped through the lobby and the first floor, flitting from mind to mind, quickly dismissing the sleeping and unguarded.

I found her on the third floor. Alone.

She lay in a bathtub of warm water and bubbles. She'd had too many meetings and too many after-dinner drinks. She felt relaxed, warm, and sexy. I entered her slowly, feeling her surround me.

She missed someone and she thought of him. I toyed with her desire, amplifying it. She massaged herself with a warm washcloth, rubbing it under her heavy breasts and across her thick nipples. They grew hard and painfully tight.

Her hand strayed lower, down her abdomen and through the thick mat of her pubic hair to the outer lips of her vagina. She stroked them gently, pushed her finger between them, and found the hard knot of her clitoris. She spread her legs wider, sliding lower in the tub.

I felt warmth spread through her as she massaged

Michael Bracken

herself, felt the electrical tingles as she began to come in the bathtub, felt the pain as her hips bucked up and down against the porcelain tub. Bubbles spilled onto the tile floor.

Orgasm overwhelmed her, swept her into ecstasy, rippled through her body like never before. She fought against unconsciousness as I grabbed the orgasm and twisted it beyond the breaking point.

Then I pulled away quickly; returned to my room to find myself bathed in sweat, my abdomen covered with semen, my own lungs gasping for air. I waited until my heart stopped pounding before pushing myself off the bed. Then I stumbled into the bathroom and stood under the icy needles of a cold shower.

I slept restlessly that night, spinning in the lumpy double bed and twisting the cotton top sheet around my thick legs. An hour after I'd given up all hope of sleep, I sat behind the wheel of the rented Ford. My plane to Chicago wasn't scheduled to leave Lambert Field until early afternoon; I had all morning to kill.

At first I drove aimlessly through the downtown streets west of the hotel. Then, as the sun rose behind the Gateway Arch, I found myself on Broadway, headed south toward the brewery. Downtown disappeared as I crossed under Highway 40 and entered Soulard. I turned at the Soulard Farmers Market, the Ford's steering wheel jerking under my hands as I drove west on the cobblestones. In the market, farmers unloaded produce, preparing their stalls for the day. I didn't stop to watch.

There's a dead zone between Soulard and Lafayette Square, a section of the city only a few blocks wide where the urban pioneers and their rehabbing fad had not dared to venture. I'd driven through it almost every time I visited St. Louis. This time I drove through, circled around, and brought the car to a halt.

Canvas Bleeding

Across the street from where I sat, the abandoned City Hospital loomed over the Malcolm Bliss Mental Health Center. Something special existed inside Malcolm Bliss, something I could not find on the street, something I had never dared to explore before.

I licked my lips as I stared at the building. Then slowly, tentatively, I scanned the people entering Malcolm Bliss. I skipped through the nurses and doctors, raced through the aides and orderlies, accelerated through the janitors and cooks and maintenance staff. They weren't what I wanted.

I wiped a sheen of perspiration off my forehead. Then I looked at my fingers, saw the sweat glisten, and felt a shiver race down my spine.

I went in.

At first I found only blanks, minds where no emotion existed. They held nothing I could grasp, nothing to amplify. I skittered away.

I found others lethargic; dull, dim-witted people unable to care for themselves and barely able to cultivate simple emotion. Their emotions were simple on/off switches, unlike the complex volume controls I usually found.

As I hurried from one mind to the next — quickly finding each emotional center, judging it, finding it lacking, and moving on — I raced through a mind that stopped me.

The man's mind was jumbled, out of control, the emotions skewing up and down the emotional range. I twisted an emotion as high as it went and tried to hold it there.

It slipped from my grasp.

I waited. Anger came up on its own, tainted with hatred and bits of emotions I couldn't identify.

He opened his eyes and stared at the broad back of a nurse. Glare from the white uniform irritated his eyes; slobber dripped silently onto his chest. When the nurse turned around, he grabbed her throat in one hand and tried to choke her. Ebony skin bulged between his pale fingers.

The nurse batted his hand away with one thick black fist. "Ain't gonna take no more of that," she said. "Ain't gonna take no more."

He shoved himself off the bed and leapt at her. The nurse outweighed him by a hundred and fifty pounds and she easily threw him back on the bed.

His emotions turned to mush. Anger disappeared. He lay quietly.

"That's better," she said. She smiled at him, her yellow teeth peeking between her thick lips.

I pulled away from the man in the bed. He was too small, too weak, with emotions too hard to control.

I slid through the nurse's mind. I left her with no alteration and scanned down the hall.

I collided with another mind.

It held broken glass and barbed wire, sharp needles, razors, butcher knives. It held Napalm and acid slowly burning eyes from their sockets. It held flaming crosses and black men with broken necks swinging from tree limbs. It held Jews and the smell of flesh-burning ovens. It held Jim Jones, Charles Manson, and John Wayne Gacy. It held hatred, fear, anger, and loathing, all amplified past rationality. It was all there before I arrived and it blew me back to the car.

Sweat stung my eyes and I tried to wipe it away. My arms shook so violently I couldn't lift them. I gulped stale air. My heart palpitated. My head felt about to explode. I'd bitten my tongue and I tasted blood.

Canvas Bleeding

Somewhere inside Malcolm Bliss existed a mind already far past anything I'd ever experienced. Somewhere inside Malcolm Bliss existed the kind of mind I'd sought for years, never able to find it.

The lonely woman on the third floor of the hotel had been a small diversion, giving a moment's pleasure. The pudgy young housewife with the laundry and the baby had been like a cheap carnival ride: the thrill only lasted a minute. I'd been looking for more: like a drug addict seeking a bigger dose each time he needed a fix, I had searched for something I couldn't get.

Somewhere inside Malcolm Bliss was what I'd been seeking: the ultimate thrill ride, a mind already pushed to the limits. I'd found it, and I feared it, and it really didn't matter because the body was securely restrained.

I sat and stared at the building for a long, long time.

Then I started the Ford and drove to the hotel to pack.

I spent a week in Chicago before they put me back on the road. I visited the student newspaper at the University of Iowa, then went east to a printing company in Springfield, Illinois. By the time I returned to St. Louis I'd sold another half million dollars worth of typesetting equipment and I'd spent at least a dozen sleepless nights thinking of what I'd found inside Malcolm Bliss.

During that month of travel, I'd looked for something similar in the towns and cities I visited. I'd come close only twice, once in a holdover cell in the Madison County jail and once in the English department of a small university. Both minds were borderline but only one was dangerous on its own.

A few hours after unpacking my bags in St. Louis, I

sat in a rented Chevrolet across the street from Malcolm Bliss. I quickly found the mind I wanted, tuned into it, and waited.

The emotions ran at full volume, relentless and unwavering. I felt them, trying to understand how they'd gotten that way, why they stayed that way, and what I could do to another mind to make it the same.

She lay in her bed staring upward while I waded through the emotional cesspool. Rage at full volume: she hated everything and everyone and hated the fact that she lay confined to her bed.

A wide black face interrupted her view of the ceiling.

"You doing all right today, Miss Emma?" asked the nurse I'd seen before. "You sure do have the most violent eyes, yes ma'am."

Miss Emma said nothing. I grabbed hatred, tried to twist the volume control, and found it broken at full volume.

Her emotions flickered as if she'd recognized the intrusion. Then nuclear holocaust erupted; a million bloated Ethiopians exploded like ruptured pimples; crosses burned on the lawns of black families across America while ebony children cried and white men laughed.

The nurse grabbed Miss Emma's shoulders and easily rolled her onto her side to stare at the window. Miss Emma's body — a husk of use only to keep the brain alive — lay paralyzed. Self-pity swam through oceans of gasoline, walked through the fires of hell, burned the death of Auschwitz.

It didn't matter to me then. Only understanding mattered.

I felt as if I'd met the beast of Revelation.

When I finally withdrew, my head tingled with thousands of tiny electrical jolts. The feeling didn't leave until I'd killed half a bottle of Jim Beam.

Canvas Bleeding

I spent the next week in meetings with two potential clients. During the hours between meetings I watched people. I scanned minds in the Central West End and in Forest Park. I scanned minds in Soulard and in Clayton. I scanned minds on the Hill and on the Riverfront.

I was parked at an apartment complex when I saw him: big, with broad shoulders and thick, muscular arms; pale brown hair curled around his ears; and violent eyes.

He walked past the car without seeing me. My head tingled as I tuned into him, quickly finding his emotional center. He seethed.

He stormed up the stairs to a second floor apartment, shoved the door open, and slammed it shut behind him. Glass doors rattled on a gun cabinet as he crashed through the apartment to the bedroom.

"They fired me," he said to the woman on the bed. "What the fuck did I ever do to them?"

The pale blonde lay mute, staring up at him. She held the covers to her neck.

"Tell me," he yelled. "What did I ever do?"

He grabbed the covers and jerked them off the bed. She wore only a black teddy.

"And what the hell are you doing in bed at two in the afternoon?"

"John, I —"

The front door of the apartment opened, then closed quietly. A male voice called, "Barbra?"

John stepped toward the night stand, pulled open the single drawer, reached in, and came away with his thick fist wrapped around a .38.

A young man stepped into the bedroom, his shirt half off, his arms caught in the sleeves.

John hesitated.

189

Michael Bracken

I twisted.

John pulled the trigger. The young man's chest exploded and he slumped against the door frame.

John spun back to his wife. Her mouth moved, but she didn't speak. He grabbed her hair and pulled her to her feet. She struggled. He backhanded her with the barrel of the revolver. A long streak of blood appeared on her cheek. She put her hands to her face. Blood oozed between her fingers. John pulled the teddy off her, discarding the wisp of blackness under his feet. He shoved her against the wall and pressed the .38 into her crotch. He squeezed the trigger. She screamed and doubled over. He pressed the barrel of the revolver against her temple and squeezed the trigger again. Her head erupted in a fountain of blood. Her body spasmed as it fell to the floor.

John stepped over his wife's body. He crossed the room. He kicked over the body in the doorway, then stepped on the dead man's face, crushing nasal cartilage.

In the living room, John unlocked his gun case. He reloaded the .38, picked out a rifle and a shotgun and loaded them. Then he stuffed his pockets full of ammunition, slung the rifle over his shoulder, stuffed the .38 into the waistband of his jeans, and headed out of the apartment and down the stairs with the shotgun in his hand.

An elderly woman shuffled out of a downstairs apartment, squinted at him through her bifocals, and said, "What was all that noise upstairs?"

John rammed the butt of the shotgun into her false teeth. A tiny Pekinese ran out of the old woman's apartment and yapped at his heels. He kicked it into the wall of the apartment building, breaking its neck.

Sirens wailed in the distance. John turned toward the sound and saw the rented Chevrolet where I sat.

He dismissed me. Through his eyes I appeared to have passed out: my head lolled back on the seat, my face gleamed with sweat. He walked past the Chevrolet, across the parking lot to a pickup truck.

He slid the rifle onto the seat, then climbed in. The sirens grew louder. The truck's engine roared to life. John dropped the truck into gear, then propped the barrel of the shotgun on the driver's door, only an inch of it showing through the open window.

He let the pickup roll forward. As he drove out of the parking lot, a police cruiser came in. One barrel of the shotgun exploded and the cop disintegrated, thousands of tiny blood stains spattering the inside of the cruiser.

John pulled the shotgun back inside the pickup as the police cruiser bumped out of control over the curb, crushing the old woman against the apartment building.

John smiled. The day had finally begun to go his way. A sense of satisfaction settled tentatively over the top of his other emotions. I let it stay a moment before I brushed it away. I couldn't allow John to be satisfied with what he'd done. There was so much more he was capable of.

When the guard at the plant where John had worked wouldn't open the gate, John pumped the other shotgun shell into his chest and crashed his pickup through.

Ahead lay a long grey building surrounded by the asphalt expanse of a half-empty parking lot. The pickup careened off a Toyota and skidded to a stop at the building's entrance. John jumped out of the truck with the shotgun in his hands. He broke it open and replaced the two spent shells. Then he slung the rifle over his shoulder and marched up the marble steps, through the glass doors, and into the building.

Michael Bracken

The receptionist looked up in surprise, her manicured fingers poised above the switchboard. A hint of lust swept through John's mind. I knocked it aside. John slammed a fist into her face, knocking her backward, away from the switchboard. She screamed. He pulled the .38 from his waistband and drilled a hole through her forehead with a single shot.

With the shotgun in his left hand and the .38 in his right, John headed down a long hallway. A door on his left jerked open and a bald-headed man stuck his head out. When he saw John, he tried to pull back in. He wasn't fast enough. John fired the .38 point-blank into the man's face.

Women began screaming. The sound came from behind him. They had discovered the receptionist.

John marched quickly down the hall toward the closed door of the company president's office. No one tried to stop him. He glanced through open doors as he passed other offices, the corner of his eye noticing a secretary hiding behind a desk in one, a middle-aged man in a blue suit crouched behind a filing cabinet in another.

He kicked open the door at the end of the hall. The company president sat impassively behind his desk, a telephone receiver pressed to one ear. Color drained from his face.

"I'll call you back," he said slowly. He licked his thick lips. His heavy jowls shook. "Something important has come up."

The company president slowly lowered the receiver.

"I want my job back," John said.

The man behind the desk cleared his throat. "I —"

"I want you to get on your knees and beg me to take my job back."

"I —" The president's face shined with sweat. "Perhaps I was a bit hasty this morning."

Canvas Bleeding

John advanced until only an oak desk separated the two men. Outside the building police sirens destroyed the quiet afternoon.

"Perhaps a mistake was made —"

"A mistake?" John interrupted. "You're damn right there was a mistake. I worked here for ten god-damned years."

"Personnel said there was some problem with attitude."

"Personnel wouldn't know a cunt from a shithouse."

"I . . . I'm sure they don't. If you would just give me the opportunity to have your file sent in, perhaps we could —"

"Don't fuck with me," John said. "You ain't got the time."

Footsteps reverberated in the hall. A police siren wailed outside the building. John moved to the window to look through a gap in the heavy curtains.

A chair crashed to the floor. John spun around to see the fat man running for the door. He pulled both triggers on the shotgun. The company president erupted in a shower of blood.

A cop in a flack jacket stepped into the room and leveled a .357. I tried to pull away. The cop squeezed the trigger. I pulled back with every ounce of strength I had. I needed time. The cop's bullet arrived. The side of John's head exploded. I felt the impact, the pain, and then I broke free.

As I sat in the rented car, my brain tingled. I tried to catch my breath, wanted to wipe my forehead, lost control of my bladder. I sat in warm urine, unable to move.

My brain burned, my eyes felt the pain of a hundred needles, my body the Napalm of a thousand Vietnams, and I tried to scream. I tried to scream for an eternity

Michael Bracken

and when I opened my eyes, I slowly focused on a familiar black face.

"You just like Miss Emma," she said as she rolled me onto my stomach and the hatred of a million tortured souls swelled within me.

About the Author

Michael Bracken is the editor of *Fedora: Private Eyes and Tough Guys* and the author of *All White Girls, Bad Girls, Deadly Campaign, Even Roses Bleed, In the Town of Dreams Unborn and Memories Dying, Just in Time for Love, Psi Cops, Tequila Sunrise,* and more than 700 shorter works published in Australia, Canada, China, England, Ireland, and the United States. He was born in Canton, Ohio, has traveled extensively throughout the U.S., and currently resides in Waco, Texas, with his wife, Sharon, and his son, Ian. He has three other children — Ryan, Courtney, and Nigel — from a previous marriage.

3 1221 06845 4813

Printed in the United States
837000001B